THE STRANGER WHO STEPPED OUT OF MY DREAMS

THE STRANGER WHO STEPPED OUT OF MY DREAMS

AMIRAL LEE

Like vintage wine,
She stood the test of time.

PARTRIDGE

To order additional copies of this book, contact
Toll Free 800 101 2657 (Singapore)
Toll Free 1 800 81 7340 (Malaysia)
orders.singapore@partridgepublishing.com

www.partridgepublishing.com/singapore

Contents

This book is dedicated to everyone involved in the completion of this novel. With this support and determination, I was able to complete a long-awaited novel in English. The story of Ashman is a fiction and does not depict any person living or dead; any resemblances are purely coincidental.

Prologue

Ashman Mohamed Ali is a man who has seen life. Born and bred in Petaling Jaya, a residential enclave which is away from the hustle and bustle from the city of Kuala Lumpur, Malaysia, he had his early education in Bukit Bintang Boys Secondary School, PJ, before pursuing his tertiary education at John Moores University in Liverpool. As a self-proclaimed Liverpudlian, he supported Liverpool Football Club over the neighbours Everton FC. His obtained a first degree in civil engineering with distinction in transportation engineering, and he started his career with Straits Steamship Co. Ltd. in Liverpool. Upon his return to Malaysia, he joined the United Engineering Berhad until his retirement.

As an accomplished professional and in his personal life, he had his ups and downs. To begin with, he met his childhood heart-throb Ashfah Abu Bakar, in the Section 11 neighbourhood of Petaling Jaya. Love blossomed when both attended a Christmas Eve dinner at a friend's house. He then proposed to her after a whirlwind romance which lasted three months, by which Ashfah would have completed her studies at the nearby University of Malaya. The rest, as they say, is history. They were married in a very simple ceremony at Ashfah's residence minus all the razzmatazz.

After the fairytale romance and being elevated to a married life situation, the honeymoon days were soon over.

They were blessed with their only daughter, Ashley, but it was Ashfah who drew the first blood, and their marriage was almost ruined. Confounded by a burst of speed to acquire riches from the wheeling and dealing in real estate profession, she found solace in the arms of another man, who soon proved to be a thorn in their otherwise happy marriage. This led to their break-up in their thirteen-year marriage, and a new future was charted for them. Not in their wildest imaginations would they have thought they'd be ending the marriage in the Syariah court, and it was a stormy divorce after a series of hearings.

Soon after the split, Ashman found time for travelling, something that always eluded him due to work commitments, and he also browsed social media for friends old and new. On Facebook, he befriended Azmah Abdul Aziz, a former stewardess and homemaker from Batu Pahat, Johor and one day they decided to meet up. The rendezvous was at Petaling Jaya Hilton, and Azmah took her friend along to introduce to him, but instead Ashman fell for Azmah head over heels. She treated him like a friend initially, but later she became close to him as he confided in her and confessed his feelings. However, she took it with an open heart while she remained faithful to her husband, who was not in the best of health. It was love at the first sight for him, and as he'd indicated earlier to her, if she became available, then his plan would proceed. It was a long and winding courtship, and Ashman registered his interest in a buyout clause in Azmah's marriage.

Selling the idea of a buyout clause was nothing new, and they were performed in the past under various guises, but the morality of it was at stake. Undeterred by the methods exercised earlier, Ashman explored a number of possibilities after consulting the Syariah experts. Unlike buyout clauses in professional soccer or the Shiite way of a mutaah, a buyout clause would only be to register a first option in asking for Azmah's hand should she be free from any encumbrances. Her ailing husband was like a cloud with a silver lining for both of them to tie the matrimonial knot. In the interim, Azmah remained loyal to her ailing husband and performed her duties as a wife. Her two grown-up boys initially did not take kindly to such arrangements. With Ashman's wit and diplomacy, eventually her two sons came around to the idea of a replacement for their father and accepted him in good faith.

As the heavens were to dictate, Azmah's husband, Azman Ali, passed away peacefully in Kota Damansara. All was quiet on the Western front for a while. After the edah period of four months and ten days for a Muslim widow, romance was once again in the air, and the lovebirds took a more holistic approach towards life and in particular their matrimonial plan. Prior to that, they both performed the pilgrimage, or haj, together in 2013, with Ashman suddenly getting the call-up from Tabung Haji, the Government Pilgrimage Board, after registering in 2009. It was a memorable trip for both of them, especially the ascension of Jabal Rahmah, the very place that Adam met Eve again after descending to earth. This was the most preferred place to visit as a symbol of eternal love. Others milestones were the special payers in Arafah, the visit to the Prophet Muhammed's (PBUH) Mausoluem, and last but not least the Warriors Cemetery at Jabal Uhud in Medinah.

The return from haj, though on different flights, was a start to another chapter in their lives. After the departure of her husband, Azman Ali, she then related her haj experiences to her parents. Azmah then slotted her intention to tie the matrimonial knot again, as a Muslim widow would aspire for the replacement of a life companion. Though her aspirations were noble and her words were carefully deciphered, there was a strong objection from her autocratic father, who had a final say as a wali, or guardian, in giving away his daughter. She was disappointed in the objections from her father, but her two sons were a source of strength, and Azmah soon faced the dilemma of a conflict between her father and her newfound love. As a woman of substance, she would not easily throw in the towel. The plot then thickened.

Ashman brought his Syariah lawyers to the fore, and the battle would soon be set with two options opened: either bring his father-in-law in waiting to court for refusal to agree to the marriage, or perform marriage outside the state or country without the need for the wali's approval. After much consultation, the latter would be the preferred option for him, and Perlis seemed a likely destination for the marriage solemnisation. After having done due diligence on this move, it was all systems go. The stage was set, and the State Religious Department was a stone's throw from the hotel where Ashman and his group checked in the evening before. However, disaster struck before the Subuh prayers: a commando-style abduction took place at Zaini's residence, where Azmah was putting up, and she was carried to a waiting car, leaving the rest in shock and disbelief.

A fairytale ending was not written in the stars, and Azmah spent her final years in solitary confinement enforced by her autocratic father. The proliferation of anxiety, embarrassment, upset, and broken-hearted precipitated into severe depression. It was too much for her to bear, and she developed Alzheimer's as she fell from grace. Azmah rejected all other proposers in asking for her hand as advocated by her father.

It was now 2015, and the latest development took a new twist. After consultation with Ashman and her two sons, she took a bold decision to be admitted to the dementia nursing home in Teluk Panglima Garang, Banting, Selangor. The powers that be finally granted her last wish. Her two sons and Ashman obliged and respected her decision for the treatment she needed. Another Natrah or the Bertha Hertogh saga in the making, or another fairytale ending of happily ever after? The last chapter provides an explosive moment with high emotions, and readers will find it intriguing and difficult to resist reading till the end.

Chapter 1

Ice Cream Bells, Church Bells, and Wedding Bells

In the early seventies, ice cream was a local favourite either as a dessert or a starter, or even as a meal to those who had tonsillitis. But in the locality of Section 11, Petaling Jaya, some neighbours would stop the seller on a motorbike under some shady trees to savour its taste. This was the time when Ashman, a local resident, would come out to briefly meet other neighbours and friends for a short hang-out. There were a number of regular customers, but his focus was more on a petite young lass who lived down the street and was much younger than him, likely in his early teens. By this time, Ashman (or Ash to friends) was doing his A level equivalent at the Mara Institute of Technology after completing his studies at Bukit Bintang Boys Secondary School in Jalan Utara, PJ.

One fine afternoon, Ashman was determined to buy Ashfah an ice cream, and he waited for her to show up at the ice cream cart. As it worked out, Ashfah came out from the nearby Assunta Secondary School in Jalan Changgai to savour some ice cream before heading home. Ashman was so delightful that his first hello to her came out with a bang. "A special ice cream for you on this hot and beautiful day?"

"Thank you. How nice of you," came the reply. "What's the big occasion?" he asked her.

Ashman was at a loss for words. Eventually his reply was, "I know you love ice cream." Short and concise – that was the epoch-making encounter between Ashman Mohamed Ali and Ashfah Abu Bakar.

It wasn't too long before they became close friends and distant neighbours in the locality. Ashfah, also known as Ash to her friends, is the second daughter of a police inspector attached to the PJ police district in Jalan Penchala. She was of mixed parentage because her mother was a Banjar Malay from Teluk Intan, Perak and her father was of Portuguese descent from Malacca and converted to Islam during marriage. Her friendship was informally approved by Ashfah's parents, who did some homework on Ashman's background. Ashman came from a respected middle-income family whose father hailed from Pattani, Thailand, and her mother was a local resident. Both were businesspersons in their own rights. The parents of Ashman and Ashfah didn't have big families, and Ashman only had an elder brother, working at *New Straits Times* as a junior journalist. The neighbourhood of Section 11 was a busy but friendly fraternity.

They seemed to be childhood friends, but Ashman is seven years older than Ashfah, and it initially looked like a big brother and sister relationship. Nonetheless, they looked more like normal friends rather than anything else. Ashman would still remember the song by Conway Twitty, "Don't Cry Joni".

"Jimmy, Jimmy, please wait for me".
"I grow up someday, you see",

"Saving my kisses just for you..."
"Joni, Joni, please don't cry".
"You forget me by and by",
"You are fifteen, and I am twenty-two",
"Joni, I just can't wait for you".

How touching were those lyrics? Even now, in his armchair, he could rekindle those halcyon days of yore. He even kept an old vinyl long-play record, or LP, of Conway Twitty, and he would play it over and over again with his classic turntable. As an audiophile who loved high fidelity music, he also played the guitar and would serenade a few songs to her whenever she visited him.

As time flew by, Ashman completed his A levels from the Mara Institute of Technology in Section 17. As he prepared to plan his future, his father would ask him what he would pursue as a career. As a Liverpool FC fan, he would love to go to Liverpool to further his studies.

"Tell me what you want to be," said his father.

Ashman had a passion for trains, ships, and automobiles, and his toys during his young days has been models. "I'd like to pursue a career in transportation," was his reply. The next logical step to take was to apply for admission to a course in transportation engineering. This course of study was available at John Moores University in the city of Liverpool. His mum would prefer he go to London, where Malaysian food was easily available, but nonetheless it was all's well that ends well.

The song continued with,

"Soon I left our little hometown,
Get a job and try to settle down."

3

There was little time left to bid farewell to close relations and friends, and Ashman was given one week to report to John Moores University, Liverpool, as a freshman. It was a rush job all along, and for admission, thankfully the student visa was ready on time. Ashfah helped as she could, and each passing day before the departure, it was like a clock ticking away the minutes. Indeed, Einstein's theory of relativity was put to test.

The flight on Malaysian Airlines cost RM2150 on list price, but his dad got it for a half the amount courtesy of a friend at a travel agency. Ashfah was at the Subang International Airport to see him off on a Saturday evening flight for London, and she hoped that after O levels, she could be a flight stewardess to be in touch with Ashman.

After all the family hugs and before entering the departure hall, Ashman still had time to ask her where the word *pramugari* originated from. Her only answer was *stewardess* in the Malay language. Ashman kept her guessing until the announcement for boarding was made. He told her that *pramugari* was an Indonesian acronym for PRA, which meant Penyambut. MU was Tetamu, GA was Garuda Airways, and RI was Republic Indonesia. In short, pramugari was an acronym in the Malay and Indonesian language for guest relations staff for Garuda Airways.

Liverpool had always been Ashman's preferred destination to live, study, and possibly work after graduation. He settled down quickly in the city of the Beatles. Apart from studying, he would go to Anfield Stadium on match days to watch his favourite players like Kevin Keegan, Ray Clemence, and Emelyn Hughes, to name a few. The city had a number of eateries serving Halal Muslim food, particularly from Pakistan and the Middle East. The winter of 1974 was very cold and was one of the worst in many years. There was this Malaysian community in Toxteth, Liverpool that was home to Malaysian sailors, particularly from Straits Steamship Co. Upon their retirement, they did not want to go back. Ashman made himself at home in the community and made friends with some of them.

The first mail from Ashman reached Ashfah less than a fortnight later after he'd settled down. A phone call preceded the letter soon after he reached Heathrow Airport. Ashman took a train ride to Liverpool from the Euston Road station and reached the Lime Street station in Merseyside. The first portion of the letter was penned during the journey. His opening words read,

"My dear Ash, I hope you do not miss me, because I am going to send you letters during my stay in Liverpool."

Those opening words left tears in her eyes like raindrops from the sky, but as a strong-willed person, she took it in stride. Her father advised her not to drool too much over the matter and concentrate more on her studies, because she would be sitting her lower certificate examination in a couple of months. She was an obedient daughter, and it was a like a panacea for all the sorrow.

After a series of letters and occasional phone calls, gradually the mail was less frequent, and phone calls were few and far in between. Ashfah thought this was his first-year examination and understood his actions, but life went on for the young lass of PJ, and she would sit her O Levels soon. She did receive a good-luck card from him and that was enough for her. Ashfah completed her O Levels exam with a second grade but her dying ambition to be a flight stewardess met a mixed reaction from her parents, who wanted her to continue studies at A Levels and pursue tertiary education at the nearby University of Malaya. Again she obliged her parents because she was daddy's girl. Soon after that, Ashfah gained admission to the University of Malaya and did a three-year degree programme in humanities.

Back in Liverpool, Ashman was going through his final exams in the summer of 1978. He obtained a degree in civil engineering and waited for the convocation ceremony before returning to Malaysia. The much-awaited return to his motherland was like a father expecting his first child. Aside from a brief return two years earlier during the semester break in the summer of 1976, this return would reunite with all with a fait accompli, and he bore the "BSc in civil engineering" following his name.

For Ashfah, it was her second year at UM, and this was the moment she'd been waiting for. Time stood till for Ashfah when Ashman was warmly received at the Subang International Airport. Though there was no standing ovation for him, there were a few minutes of silence after he walked out of the departure hall. The first words from him to her were, "Hi, I am back." After all the handshakes, the party headed towards Sri Yazmin Restaurant in Ampang Park, where they dined. All the stories of the wonderful stay in the UK took up all of dinner time. After the relaxation at the cosy restaurant, a cultural show was the most fitting occasion to the evening. Ashman then broke the news that he had a job offer with Straits Steamship at its headquarters in Liverpool, and he would return a month later.

The news was received with mixed feelings from all, but it was much to the chagrin of Ashfah, who had hoped for a reunion with her childhood sweetheart. Ashman didn't get the indication that all along, Ashfah was waiting for him; to him, she was no more than a close friend. After some explanation from him, Ashfah understood his desire to gain international working experience for a couple of years before returning home with better credentials. This was a golden opportunity not to be missed. It was thanks to Ibrahim for introducing him to the managing director of the shipping company while in Kampung Malaysia, Toxteth.

Fast forward a couple of years on. Ashman completed his two-plus years stint in Liverpool and was now back in Malaysia for good. He was still single. His mum and dad were delighted, and Ashfah was delirious with joy upon his return. Her prayers for a reunion was answered. It was not that Ashfah didn't have any admirers during the period, but her strong hopes of being with Ashman again superseded everything. She totally forgot the remaining lyrics of the song by Conway Twitty, which read,

"Jimmy, Jimmy, please don't cry.
You will forget me by and by.
It's been five years since you're gone.
Jimmy, I married your best friend, John."

Back again in the family house of Mohamed Ali, Ashman spend a few days to recover from the jet lag. Then it was back to job hunting for the Liverpool-trained lad. Meanwhile, his passion for music never faded, and now it was time to listen to the old vinyls of yesteryears in his bedroom. The Beatles seemed to be his favourite, but other groups like ABBA were contemporary to the times. While listening to some soft music, a phone call for Ashfah came. The couple spent the afternoon hooked on the line. By now the muezzin's call for the Asar prayer took centre stage, and after the prayers went another day.

One Sunday, Ashman was awakened by the nearby church bells at St Paul's Church, along the nearby Jalan Utara. He had been living in Section 11 since his young days, and church bells were nothing new on Sundays. But this church bell reminded him of some years ago when, upon hearing the church bell, he and Ashfah would meet at the bus stop shelter at the same Jalan Utara to take a ride on the Sri Jaya buses, either to PJ New Town or to Kuala Lumpur. Images of him and her during their young days suddenly popped up to his mind. That was to be their first date in the puppy-love days. He would take her for a movie in the Coliseum Theatre, and then they'd have a meal together at the nearby restaurant. Those memorable days would never cease to be on his mind, even after a gap of several years being abroad.

Those were the days Ashman treasured all the memories, and he recollected some events with nostalgia. On one occasion, he would take her to the nearby Lake Taman Jaya in the evening and watched all the birds that nestled amongst the many trees. Up to this day, Ashman still wondered what future lies for him regarding his relationship with Ashfah. He didn't have many female friends around, and all of them were casual friends. Ashfah seemed closest to him so far, but not close enough to confide in certain matters. Perhaps he thought that with such an age difference, she may not be able to share feelings with him.

Ashman then did some soul searching as to why the chemistry didn't work with her so far, or why he lacked the kind of push to make it happen. His dad was a quiet person and wouldn't talk to him much about this unless time was of the essence. Instead, mum would occasionally bring up the subject, but so far it was too early to be brought to discussion. It might be that the time was not suitable enough to discuss the matter, but Ashman still had to land a job.

Not long after, Ashman was offered a position with United Engineering Berhad, in the project development division. His employers were impressed by his credentials. The first office was at the nearby, Petaling Jaya, a few kilometres from his house. By now he was able to afford to have his first car, a Ford Cortina Ghia. Of course his first ride on the car was with her, and it was she who chose the colour of the car, a silver metallic. By now they were seen together more often, and occasionally he drove her to the varsity because she was in the final year of her studies. It seemed that love would blossom between the two.

Now Ashman felt that the chemistry with her was developing thanks to his mum, who played a pivotal role in giving him the push that was required. With the car, it would be easier for him to take her around, and he would be warmly received by her parents. On one occasion, he offered her family a lift to Kuala Lumpur because her dad's car was out of service. This proved to be a turning point in their relationship and was a hint of things to come.

By now Ashfah had completed her final year exams, and after the convocation ceremony at the Dewan Tunku Chancellor, life for her was more exciting because studies were now over. Not long afterwards, she was offered employment at the Ministry of Labour in Kuala Lumpur. Now the time was set that Ashman would have to make an announcement to his family that he was now ready to propose to her and tie the matrimonial knot.

In one candlelit dinner at PJ Hilton, he proposed to her. Following that, a small evening tea was held at Ashfah's house. Ashman's parents also attended the occasion to come to a gentleman's agreement and finalise some arrangements.

All in all, it took about a fortnight to make it happen. The consensus was reached, and both parties decided to have a small do. The marriage solemnization took place at her house, and the following day there was an afternoon reception attended by close relatives and friends numbering approximately one hundred in number.

Chapter 2

Days of Wine and Roses

Like the evergreen song of the above namesake, sung by Andy Williams, Ashman and Ashfah were married in a simple ceremony and reception, with no razzmatazz like some other weddings. They saved enough money for a short honeymoon. The destinations thought of included Liverpool, Perth, and nearby places like Bali and Phuket. Phuket was the preferred destination for the newlyweds because both of them didn't set foot as of yet, and it was also a destination proposed by his father, whose immediate ancestors were from Thailand. It was a short notice to their respective employers to ask for a short break. The sunny sunshine and the best sunset, as advertised of Phuket from the Tourist Organisation of Thailand, or TOT, interested the young couple. They packed their bags and headed north via a flight in Penang.

Upon arrival in Phuket, in the afternoon the couple wasted no time heading to the beaches to bask in the tropical sun. By evening they were back to the hotel and were truly exhausted. The following morning, they were treated to breakfast in bed. After breakfast, they decided to stroll around the hotel beach, and they later took a ride to town for some window shopping. They bought a few souvenirs of the island. In the afternoon was a foot massage session at the hotel. The evening was free and leisurely, killing time before dinner. At the hotel, they were treated to a sumptuous dinner spread and entertainment via the hotel's resident musical band. Ashman volunteered to go on stage and crooned the song "Widuri", which he dedicated it to Ashfah. What an applause they received from the other guests!

The next couple of days were spent in a similar fashion, with a routine expected of a honeymoon holiday. During the stay, there was also a boat trip around the Andaman Sea, and the sunset was so beautiful and breathtaking that the islanders claimed it to be the best sunset in the world as the sun slowly sank into the horizon. What an experience that was, and the couple cherished such moments of togetherness and intimacy far from the crowds. They returned to Kuala Lumpur the following day with sweet memories of the trip.

Back in PJ, Ashman and Ashfah were busy at work, and their evenings were filled with invitations by relatives to get to know them. This went on for a month, and by now the honeymoon was over.

In her first few months of work, Ashman would send her to work at the Jalan Duta government offices, and later to his place of work in the evening. The thoughts of having another car for her arose, but she had to wait for a couple of months before her government car loan became available. It was the routine kind of commute to two different destinations for him. On certain occasion, she would get a lift from her office colleagues when he could not make it due to work commitments.

Her first car was a Proton Saga 1.5S, and the down payment was from Ashman. Now that he could stay in the office slightly longer to complete job assignments, it didn't go down well with her, but she was a headstrong person who could withstand all the rigours of being on her own. Ashman's presence would have helped her at home, but he was mostly in the office, completing project assignments and meeting tough datelines. For him, when the going got tough, the tough got going! Such was their early working lifestyles. There were times when his United Engineering Berhad submitted project proposers to the relevant ministries, and some key staff worked the whole night through. The theme of the group work was, "You'll never work alone."

She spent most of her waiting time listening to light, easy music, though regular chats with her in-laws filled half the boredom while awaiting for him to be back. Her favourites were the Carpenters, Whitney Houston, and the local Sharifah Aini. Occasionally she would cook for him his favourite dishes, and her in-laws also liked what she cooked. Sometimes it bon appétit when the whole family got together for a home meal. Sundays were when the family would invite close relatives or friends for a good lunch. He would take the lead by doing his own marketing at the local market at Section 14, PJ, and sometimes she would follow him. All in all, it was a family affair. There were times that return invitations filled up the other half of the weekends. Those were the days of a six-day work week.

"What would you like to have for lunch today?" asked Ashfah.

"Why don't we have lunch at Coliseum?" he answered.

"Great, let's go!"

They headed to the Coliseum for a Western culinary experience. Over at the Coliseum, there was a queue to be seated, and they waited outside for twenty minutes before securing a table for two. There they met an old buddy, Jimmy Looi, an ex–Bukit Bintang whom Ashman had not seen for almost ten years. Ironically, both had gone to the UK for further studies, but Jimmy went to Imperial College in London to do his civil engineering degree. With such a brief encounter, they exchanged name cards to catch up with each other.

Back home in PJ, Ashman and Ashfah were relaxing in the garden of the house. The Coliseum was a better place for her to break the good news to him. Her period hadn't come for the month, and after she visited the clinic a few days ago, it was confirmed that she was in the early stages of pregnancy. It was to their parents that they wanted to break the good news. All were delighted at the news of her pregnancy and gave little prayers and thanksgiving.

Ashfah was carrying, and during this time she did less of the household chores and made regular check-ups at the university hospital nearby. Towards the later part of her pregnancy, Ashman would drive her to and from work. She recited verses of the Koran during the period, praying for the safe delivery of their child. As the days advanced, the would-be father was busier than ever, preparing for his first child. Jaleel Baby Centre at New Town PJ was a one-stop centre for expectant parents to purchase necessary items. Money shouldn't be a problem for now, and all parties waited for the arrival of the newborn.

They were set for the joyful and historical day, and the baby finally arrived in July at the nearby university hospital.

It was a baby girl weighing 3.9 kilograms, and both mother and daughter were doing well. Ashman was there to say the prayers, or azan, upon receiving it from the doctor. Before that, he was carefully selecting the name for his daughter, and now he had one in his mind. Filling out the birth certificate was to be done the following day, when the forms came in. Before that, he informed her that their daughter would be named Ashley Mohamed. He wanted a surname because most Malay Malaysians did not have a surname, just a father's name. Ashley was her first name, and Mohamed was the surname derived from half his father's name, Mohamed Ali. The latest addition to the family was a bundle of joy to all.

Ashfah was on a forty-two-day maternity leave and looked after Ashley most of the time during this period. The boredom of staying home was overtaken by the joy of having the apple of her eye in the form of Ashley. Ashley was a healthy child from childbirth without any jaundice whatsoever. Ashman would often come home early from work to be with Ashley. Now they had three "Ashes" in the family. Ashley's grannies were fond of the latest addition to their grandchild, and they would pamper her, but it was to be expected.

As the months and years went by, Ashley grew up and was enrolled at the nearby kindergarten. She had a couple of friends at the pre-school level.

Back at work, Ashfah was feeling the strain as a government employee, with small pay and very little annual increases, but the demands were like those in the private sector, and of course most of the times the family was financially dependent on Ashman. For him, this was a recession period where economy slowdown was the name of the game, and most employers followed this trend. They were trying times with no salary increases, and the following year, there was even salary reduction because projects for United Engineering Berhad were difficult to secure. Indeed, these were difficult times for everyone as the country suffered from the fall of the Ringgit. However, the couple managed to take it in stride amidst the sacrifices made. As the saying goes, "There's a silver lining in every cloud."

Occasionally the couple would take Ashley for a holiday around the country, apart from visiting their relations in the kampungs, or villages from where their parents originated. Ashman had his relatives from his ancestral home in Pattani, south of Thailand, and her parents came from Perak and Malacca. There, they would spend some time catching up with their relatives and old friends, and they were treated to sumptuous meals reminiscent of the good old days. They never failed to come back with some goodies courtesy of local shops. They were such memorable trips back to their parents' hometowns.

Holidays were mostly spent at Port Dickson and Penang, with its pristine beaches. It was time to relax at those places, and at the same time they could savour some local favourite foods, especially in Penang. The best and original nasi kandar was in Penang, such as Kayu, Line Clear, and Kepala Simpang. The barbeque squids, or sotong bakar, was another favourite, followed by pasembor, or vegetable salad with peanut sauce. There were other delicacies as well. On their way back from Penang, they would stop at Kuala Kangsar for the best steamed pau, or they'd go to Tanjung

Malim. Ashley loved all those, but her favourites was Ipoh's mee rebus. Everyone had their inklings about good food and never failed to find it on those trips.

It was back to good times as the Malaysian economy recovered from the economic slowdown of the late eighties. Ashman's employers were getting projects, the PLUS Highway started, and the LRT was conceived and in its initial stages. Every employee of United Engineering Berhad was waiting for some bonus handouts towards the end of the year. Ashman received a handsome package commensurate with all the perseverance and hard work put in during the hard years.

Ashfah was glad that his patience had paid off. One day she asked, "How about a trip to Europe? I have never been there."

He paused before answering, "Yes, why not. We can bring Ashley along."

After some discussions they decided to go to London and his alma mater city of Liverpool. They were off to London by Malaysia Airlines for a ten-day stay in the two cities. It was almost autumn when they went, and it was a little cooler over there, but the English Premier League season had just started. They arrived on a Friday at Heathrow and stayed in London for four days at a cosy hotel at Bayswater near Edgware Road, where his favourite Mawar Restaurant was located. Places visited include Trafalgar Square, Piccadilly Circus, Camden Garden, and of course Buckingham Palace's changing of the guards. Ashley was happy during the entire visit to London.

The next trip was to the Merseyside, where they boarded a Virgin train at Euston Road and reached the Lime Street station in Liverpool after less than three hours. It was a pleasant journey, and upon arrival they checked in at the Travel Lodge Hotel downtown, just minutes away from the waterfront. The following day was a visit to his alma mater at John Moores University, and they followed that with dinner at a Pakistani restaurant serving Beriani rice and kebabs. On the final day of the visit, the Ashes went to Anfield Road to watch the derby against local rivals, Everton, which ended in a draw.

The following day, the Ashes return to London by the same Virgin train service and stayed there for two nights. This time the final shopping was done at factory outlet stores in Bicester, not far from London for clothes and other apparel, not to mention the souvenirs for their loved ones back home. It was a long flight back from Heathrow, London to Kuala Lumpur because of a two hour delay in London. They arrived safely at the Subang International Airport with both their parents waiting for them. It was their most memorable holiday.

Chapter 3

High Fidelity and High Infidelity

Ashman had always had a passion for good music since the days of the Beatles, and this genre of music was his favourite. But his early music belonged to the rock and roll of Elvis Presley in the early sixties and the top songs of that era, like "It's Now or Never", a hit song by the king, and of course "Oh Carol" by Neil Sedaka. Songs like "Sealed with the Kiss" by Bobby Vinton, "Mustaffa" by Bob Azzam, and "Never on Sunday" by Connie Francis had now become evergreen songs appealing to most age groups. He would collect those vinyl records and play them regularly, often serenading Ashfah. As time progressed, he would follow contemporary music, but his collection of the Beatles albums were complete then, thanks to his stay in Liverpool during his student days.

Throughout the years, he had collected over two thousand pieces of vinyl that comprised single EPs, extended play EPs, and LPs in either ten- or twelve-inch format. He would still go around the country in search of rare and limited-edition vinyls. Albums by local singers and artists, especially P. Ramlee and Saloma, were his targets then, plus others in the same era. As an audiophile, he would travel up and down the country once there was news of any availability. One of the trips was to Malacca, and the Jonker

Street was his favourite haunt for old vinyl records and antiques. Ashfah would occasionally accompany him for such trips, just to be with him during the weekends. At one juncture she moaned, "Do I have to do this for my entire life?" "Just relax, honey. What is important is that we are together," was his reply.

Soon after, the Ashes were on their way home, leaving Malacca for PJ. By now the new PLUS Highway was fully commissioned, so their journey was a breeze. During the journey back, they stopped at the Seremban R&R for a short break and helped themselves for coffee. She told him, "Stop here. I need to take a short breather at the prayer house."

So exhausted she was that the stop turned into to forty winks. He looked after Ashley and took her for a stroll around the R&R. By then the evening was approaching, and so they continued their journey to PJ. Mum prepared dinner this time, and after dinner some music was played at the behest of Dad, who joined the fray to relax. Looking tired, Ashfah headed for bed after clearing the dishes, and the men were still engrossed with the music.

Being an audiophile and anglophile, Ashman would spend a small fortune on the high fidelity, or hi-fi set, for his listening pleasure. By then, after some upgrading, his system would be all-British equipment that consisted of an Exposure 2010 integrated amplifier, Exposure 2010 power amplifier, Linn Sondek turntable with a Grado stylus, NAD phono stage, and a pair of Castle three-way floor speakers. Even the connecting wires were British to bring harmony to the system. The end result was par excellence. He had a special room to house all this, and it was fully air-conditioned with some padding on the walls for maximum effect. That was truly an audiophile room, and he spent most of his leisure time there.

Dad would occasionally pop into this room to share the enjoyment whenever he was there. Ashley also came in once in a while, but the other ladies of the house were not frequent visitors to the room, except to inform them that dinner was ready. "How much have you spent on their entire system, vinyl records, and room improvement?" asked Ashfah.

Being a down-to-earth person, Ashman replied, "Close to thirty thousand Malaysian Ringgit."

"We could have another holiday for half the amount," Ashfah said cynically.

Not wanting to prolong the issue, he remained quiet. Just to pacify her, he asked, "Why not we have some popiahs for tea at the Medan Selera?"

"Well, if you insist," she replied, knowing that it was one of her favourite light dishes for tea. He started the car and soon headed for Section 14, PJ.

Over tea and while savouring the delicious popiah from Khaleed's stall, located on the first floor of Medan Selera (gourmet's corner), she insisted that the topic for discussion should not be music.

"Ashley, tell us how school was yesterday."

Ashley was glad to tell stories of school, particularly her friends, but she wanted her mum to brief Dad on her studies, which normally occupied a quarter of the time during tea or coffee; otherwise, she would relate it at the earliest convenience to Mama Ash. Ashman was equally concerned about her studies even while listening to the music.

21

There was a need too to introduce a karaoke set within the music room. Since its inception, she had always wanted the set at home rather than crooning at the club or any karaoke centre. At last he agreed that the karaoke set had be part of the music room. As usual, he posed a question. He asked "What is the origin of the word karaoke?"

She replied, "Karaoke means singing, lah."

"That's not the answer. Karaoke originated from a Japanese word *kara*, which means without, and *oke*, which means orchestra. Singing without an orchestra is karaoke."

It didn't matter to her in the end, as long as the set was installed. That was another milestone in his passion for music, and it was a family affair too.

His penchant for music didn't stop there. By now his company had been restructured but the name of United Engineering Berhad remained. There was this celebration of two religious festivals, the Aidil Fitri Raya for Muslims and the Deepavali for the Hindus, which overlapped one another that year. A company function was to be held at lunch for all employees as a treat and a show of gratification to the staff. It was called DeepaRaya and would be held at the famous Saloma Bistro at Jalan Ampang. The highlight of the DeepaRaya was the entertainment hour with participation from staff. Every musically inclined staff member was eager to show the stuff they were made of. True to expectations, Ashman was selected to break the ice with the first song.

He was to select a duet partner to sing the first song, "Selamat Hari Raya". He chose a colleague from another department, Siti Mariam, as a partner. After a few sessions of rehearsal, the grand day came, and he was accompanied by the in-house band, called the Slim River Boys. During the entertainment hour, he delivered the song perfectly, very similarly to the original artist who'd recorded it, Hail Amir and Uji Rashid. They received applause from the audience, and a small memento were presented to them at the end of the session by their group's managing director.

But, it didn't go down well with Ashfah, who was also present. A little bit of jealously and possessiveness crept into her. However, he was quick to pacify her back home. Sometimes it was not easy to handle her, but he was more than patient in dealing with her, and their early years of being friends was a guiding factor in maintaining harmony in their relationship. Ashley was doing her part well in maintaining the balance of the relationship.

Back at work, for Ashfah it was more a mundane job in the Government Ministry of Labour, doing more administrative than frontline operations and dealing with employers and trade unions. Up till then, the pay structure in the public sector was much lower than the private counterparts. Her pay was only one-third of Ashman's, and most of her needs were supported by him. After her monthly deduction, she would purchase clothing and some food, plus a bit for Ashley from her pay. For the rest, she was dependent financially from him. Though it was not a problem for her to ask him for money, she would like some degree of financial freedom. A switch of jobs from public to private was always ruled out because he wanted her to be self-secured. A job in the private sector had its risks, and the thought of retrenchment should the economy go bad had always been in his thoughts.

"What am I doing in a place like this, without progress and promotion on the horizon?" she bemoaned.

One day she thought of having to do some part-time job which could bring extra income for her, like direct selling or real estate. The former didn't appeal to her, which left her with the latter. Within a couple of months, she met an old friend who was in the real estate business and was impressed by her monthly financial rewards. After going through a series of chats and discussions with her friend, Yasmin Yahya, Ashfah's interest intensified. The next logical step was to discuss the subject with Ashman. After a few sessions and a bedtime chat, she finally managed to convince him on the proposed part-time job.

"Please don't let this interfere with your work, and don't take too much from family time," he told her.

Upon enrolment as a part-time real estate agent, she went for a series of training sessions together with her up-line agent in KL. She took about a month to complete the course. Occasionally she would drop by the agency office in Section 51A PJ after work to keep abreast with current developments, and sometimes she'd return home as late as 10 p.m., completely exhausted. Ashley missed Mum so much that Dad took over the maternal role as well and provided comfort for her in Mum's absence.

Ashfah was reminded of meeting difficult people who would take her for a ride without closing the deal. They were the big bad wolves coming in sheep's clothing.

"Look out for those characters when meeting up with these people," he advised her."

"Not to worry, dear. I can take care of myself," she said.

The first few months of her new part-time job were tough, and she made no sales even though there were positive inquiries. Encouragement still flowed for her from her up-line leaders, but the real estate agency business was tough and very competitive. The fourth month she had a rental of an apartment, and the following month she had a sale of an apartment. The next two months drew blanks. The commission earned from the sale of the apartment were put in her savings, though it was not much, and there was a small dinner treat for the family to celebrate it. After that, sales were few and far between. She moaned,

"I never thought real estate business was this tough. It's far from what my up-line leaders said. Am I being taken for a ride?"

Balancing work as a government servant and part-time real estate was tough, let alone spending time with her family. It wouldn't be fair to her to use office time for personal business, though lots of other people did it. She wouldn't do it. Inside her office, there were others, particularly the ladies, who did direct selling under the guise of multi-level marketing, which ranged from selling cookies to cosmetics. Business rivalry was so intense that one wouldn't buy from the other for fear it would be revealed and reported to their immediate superiors.

After one year, business improved slightly for her, but it was not good enough because she was well below the targets set. At one point she almost reached her target, but the company readjusted it to a higher level. She was disappointed and angrily told her up-line. As expected her supervisor always kept a deaf ear to all these. As times she pondered how these arrangements were made with little benefit to people like her.

Ashman expressed his views.

"May be it's time for you to quit, concentrate on your full-time work, and spend more time on the family."

Ashley expressed the same concerns to her and wanted her mum to guide her in her studies. Ashfah gave her assurance that she needed another year to be involved. Pending the outcome, she would decide to stop or continue.

The second year, her business proved to be busier than ever, and more time was taken up with meeting prospective clients of all ages. Meetings with these prospective clients took place at the specific property locations and were sometimes followed by tea at restaurants and hotels. She might have to meet difficult customers who would demand lots of bonuses in order to secure a sale, and she was wary of that. So far she was able to ward off the wolves with their hidden agendas. To her surprise, one of them asked,

"How about a one-night stand to secure the deal?"

Upon hearing that, she quickly excused herself from coffee and cancelled their earlier arrangement. Feeling distraught, she took a month's leave before continuing her part-time work.

Hardcore pseudo-clients would not easily give up on their prey. They had other ways of doing it, either by working harder or a little longer, or by using some magic potions that were still prevalent in the Malay archipelagos. One day as she as having coffee at the lounge of the Crystal Crown Hotel, which was a stone's throw from her house, disaster struck. A prospective client, Noorudeen, spiked her drink, which caught her unaware. The potion didn't work instantly but moved slowly, and an illicit relationship between them developed. His promise was that she would be her sales representative in a new condominium development, and she would earn a high commission once it was fully opened for bookings. Therefore she would concentrate of meeting him after office hours, under the pretext of meeting other prospective clients. So subtle was the modus operandi that even Ashman wasn't aware of this sudden change in the frequency of meeting clients.

When Ashman was away for a couple of days on a company trip to Singapore, it was the perfect timing for Noorudeen – "when the cat is away, the mice will play". He and Ashfah would met at the Crown Princess Hotel in KL after work on 28 June in the year of the horse. They had coffee at the coffee house and talked for a while about things not at all concerning property purchase or rental. As expected, he had checked into a room earlier, and after coffee, with some coaxing, they both went up the room to freshen themselves after a hard day's work. Before entering the room, she asked,

"What's the occasion?"

His reply was, "I have something for you – just a small token for our building project."

There was a nice bracelet, which Noorudeen put on her wrist.

When he looked at her, she said, "Oh, thank you very much."

They spent the night together in the hotel room, but before that, she called Ashley to inform her that she would be back late. After that, she called her hubby to inform him. The following morning, she returned home at 6 a.m. to change her clothes and be ready for the day's work, only to realise what had happened to her. However, her illicit relationship with him continued.

Two days later, Ashman returned from Singapore and discovered from Ashley that Ashfah hadn't returned home on the fateful night. He confronted her as to why she didn't return and with whom she'd spent the night. At a loss for words, she remained silent for a while, but that didn't go down well with him. Sensing the worst could have happened, he took her out for dinner to get to the bottom of it. At last she confided in what had happened, and he had the worst shock in his life. Life wasn't the same as before for both of them.

Chapter 4

The Winter of Discontent

Ashman looked out the window to see if the rain had stopped. It rained more than one hour in the early afternoon, and he was eager to go out and play tennis at the nearby court. He said to himself, "The goes my afternoon tennis session." The rain continued to drizzle for another hour, and the weather was much cooler. He decided to stay indoors and spun a few vinyls for relaxation while the drizzle continued. There was no winter in Malaysia, but the monsoon months of October, November, and December were the coldest in the region, with temperatures ranging from 20 to 28 degrees Celsius, especially in the east coast states where the Ashes usually spent their year-end holidays.

Ashman's father came from Pattani, Thailand, and was schooled at Sultan Ismail College in Kota Bharu. In alternate years they were there to enjoy the monsoon seasons, where occasional floods were still part and parcel of the year-end holidays and the festival of the local folks. To the Ashes, it was winter time for them, and Ashley remembered vividly she and Dad took a flight to Kota Bharu for the Flood Festival. For Penangites, residents of Penang, they claimed that their year-end festival was the greatest event of the year, but in Kelantan they said that their Flood Festival was just as great.

Whoever won bragging rights was not important for Ashman, who would spend this year-end to do some soul searching. His regular mosque for prayers was the Masjid Muhhamadi, Kota Bharu. On this trip, the other Ashes did not join him. It was a difficult year for him because his dad had passed away in August, followed by his mum the following month. However, he was resilient and took everything in his stride. Ashley had been a source of inspiration for him while Mama Ash was not around. As a consolation, he would visit the few relatives left, and they would comfort him. This kind of fraternity was missing in PJ.

One evening while strolling along the Beach of Passionate Love, or PCB, he remembered the early holidays with Ashley and Mama Ash. They had a whale of a time on the beach, and the Perdana Resort Hotel nearby, where they stayed, was still fresh in his memory, as was the barbeque dinner they had at the resort's poolside. Those were memories of the good times they'd had. The ice cream seller by the name of Uncle Sam was still around, and they recognised each other. Naturally they started a conversation and had an ice cream as the evening breeze blew.

After a week's stay, Ashman headed back to PJ, and a number of assignments and tasks awaited him. Since both his parents had passed away, there were three of them in the PJ house. His elder brother stayed at Ampang Jaya. Ashfah's parents' house was half a kilometre away, and now she was contemplating moving back to her parents' house. On the instructions of her hubby, she put off the idea for a while. Ashley wasn't at all keen to move anywhere. The ripples were soon to be seen in the Ash family since the fateful night of 28 June, and Ashfah was not the same person that had been. Ashfah showed no remorse over her unfaithfulness and infidelity to Ashman, and she blamed him all along for not giving her the love she required.

Ashfah's association with and fondness for Noorudeen grew daily, as discreetly as it was. Ashman was aware of it, and this dilemma put him into a quandary. For a while the evasive Noorudeen, who hailed from Trengganu, was nowhere to be seen since the fateful night, and Ashman wasn't able to confront him. Ashfah slowly developed dislike for her hubby. She was mesmerised by the charm of Noorudeen, who by now was known to have a passion for wine, woman, and song. Ashfah gradually distanced herself from Ashman. However, this secret was uncovered by Ashfah's parents, who noticed the subtle change and advised the couple patch up for the sake of Ashley. At one point Ashfah followed her father for some cure and an alternative treatment from Darul Shifaq, but nothing positive came out of it.

"She's under someone's magic spell," said her father, trying to do some damage control.

Even at office in the ministry, her work had slackened, and her number of absences increased due to her taking leave in order to concentrate on the real estate business. Her immediate superior advised her to shape up or be shipped out. Following that, she received a warning letter from her employer, which couldn't be taken lightly. She acknowledged that letter as part of the government's General Orders procedure. She said with a grin, "Ah, to hell with the government service. I will be better off elsewhere."

For a government employee to get such a letter would be a personal insult, and that could jeopardise one's chances of a promotion to the upper echelons of public service.

As expected, she tendered her resignation from the government service after serving for more than a decade. As required in the General Orders, a three-month notice was required for confirmed employees, or in lieu of that, one month's salary would have to be paid to the government by the employee. She took the latter alternative, and only after that she did inform Ashman.

He was shocked for a moment and was speechless as to her actions. As a mitigating measure, he rushed to the ministry and met the officer in charge to hold on to the letter for a couple of days, pending his chance to persuade her to withdraw the letter. However, all was in vain because she held stubbornly to her decision – one of her traits known to family.

Ashley was equally shocked, but her expectation was that Mama Ash would quit working to spend more time with her and help her in her studies. Mum told her,

"Honey, I have to do other work to earn a living. I cannot depend on your dad alone."

What she wanted to do after quitting the government service was still not clearly identified. The promise by Noorudeen of hiring her to be his sales consultant was bullshit because he was not anywhere around; perhaps he was seeking refuge as Ashman was looking for him. In short, Ashfah changed tremendously, and she was not the same person she used to be. Ashman then remembered a quotation from William Shakespeare: "Beware of men with hooked nose and curly hair for such men are dangerous."

Back at home, there were further problems awaiting Ashman. She moved out of their bedroom and slept in the room Ashman's late parents had occupied. Young Ashley was startled and asked her dad what had happened. Ashman could only console her after a lengthy explanation. The young lass was confused, but slowly she was able to understand the situation. Luckily Ashley's grannies were near to her emotionally, and they comforted her during the difficult time. As days passed, Ashfah showed more dislike for Ashman, and there was very little in common between them. The house where they had lived happily turned out to be a monster of nightmares.

Ashfah was able to continue her part-time job at the real estate agency, and though she would be able to devote full time now, competition in this industry was intense. Her up-line leader, Yasmin Yahya, had quit and become a full-time housewife. Ashfah now was on her own, and her weakness of being taken up so easily didn't help her in her work. Sometimes she wondered, "Am I suitable for this job?" The answer had been given to her a very long time ago by none other than her hubby, but she was very adamant and ignored his advice, and she had a knack of proving otherwise. Unfortunately, it was not the case this time around.

By now she would discovered that the grass was not always greener on the other side. The industry wasn't that good at the time, and there was a downturn in the economy. She also felt the problems of it in her work. She had more free time but was unable to use it productively. As the English proverb goes, the devil works on an empty mind, and she began wondering whether a separation would be good for her. It would allow her the freedom to decide things on her own. She called her dad to discuss the matter, but it drew her a shelling. His response was so short and concise: "Think, Ashley!"

For Ashman, life at work wasn't too pleasing either. The year's end at United Engineering Berhad meant top management musical chairs were the name of the game. As usual, on 26 December, or Boxing Day, reshuffling exercises affected most employees as their bosses moved around. For Ashman, getting near the bosses was received with mixed feelings. Worse still for him, certain renowned characters were to helm his organisation. "New brooms sweep clean" was on his mind because new bosses meant different ways of doing the work, and they would bring along their own trusted confidantes. To add salt to the wound, some of them were junior not only in age and experience but also at the universities during his study days.

Realising that, Ashman tried to ask for a change of work environment after being so long with one subsidiary. He had a meeting with the head of manpower services, but his request was not going to be considered for the time being. Feeling frustrated, he walked back to his room only to find out that he had a new secretary, and she was known to be less competent. Another setback occurred at this point of his career. He moaned,

"What has happened to me?" He shook his head because there was no other way to take it. Otherwise, he might be compelled to call it quits after putting so much into the company.

Every day was like a new day at the office, with the least of surprises happening, but he was headstrong and could take it standing up. Others might have thrown in the towel.

Unless necessary, he would not stay in the office after 6 p.m., and he always looked forward to be back home with Ashley. Ashley's mum was distancing herself from him, and she didn't cook for the family anymore. Buying outside food was the only option; if Ashley wanted home-cooked food, Ashfah would bring her to her parents' house.

Since she'd moved out from their bedroom, Ashman was sleeping alone, and only his recital of the Koran relaxed him. Ashley would sleep in her own room. What was left for Ashman was the occasional visit to his music room to listen to songs. One song by Elvis,

"My Boy", was really touching:

"For your mother and me, love has finally died.

This is no happy home, but God knows how I tried.

Because of you, my boy,

You are my life, my pride, my joy.

And if I stay, I stay because of you, my boy."

Ashley meant a lot to him as the only child, and many years ago, Ashley was elected the best student at the same school as her mum.

Legally being husband and wife but having Ashfah sleep in a different room was construed as a nushus, or a disobedient wife under the Muslim Syariah law; it was regarded as marriage not consummated. As it turned out, Ashfah would use this as a strong point for her relentless pursuit of separation under the same law. Ashman tried to coax her into returning to their room, but all efforts were fruitless. Not even inviting her for a candlelit dinner with or without Ashley would mend their relationship. Ashley made attempts to have a meal together when both were at the nearby Amcorp Shopping Mall for separate purposes. Her mum was more of a guilty party, not wanting to mend the rift, and Ashley felt sad and restless at the deteriorating relationship of her beloved parents. Though she was the apple of the eye for both her parents, this was not to be her day as the only child.

Chapter 5

Ash versus Ash

As days passed by, nothing much changed for the better despite a concerted effort from Ashman and other friendly parties. Ashfah was hell-bent on going her own way. She now had a circle of friends who wrongly advised her, hoping to see the fun out of it. Career wise, there was nothing to shout about, and she remained a mediocre performer. But she was adamant and steadfast, believing she could be successful in her new career. "Has she gone bonkers?" asked one of her close friends. The same feeling was shared by Ashley, who thought that her mum had gone berserk.

Ashman was about to settle down with his new bosses, and he began to enjoy the new work style designed by his immediate superiors. After coming back from his hectic work, there was always Ashley to look forward to, and he would buy her dinner before reaching home. While on his way home after buying some Beriani rice for Ashley at Mohideen Restaurant at New Town, he noticed in the far corner of the shop Ashfah was with another two ladies, but she didn't notice him. One of the ladies was a well-known and notorious figure in the legal circles. Now it clicked his mind that this was the Syariah lawyer who'd made money out of people's misery by handling high-profile Muslim divorce cases. Her name was Yati Mansur. He soon smelt a rat from that clandestine meeting of his nushus, or estranged wife. Back home, he was trying to figure out with crossed fingers what her next move would be. In trying to do some damage control, he went over to her parents' house to discuss the matter. He reiterated what happened at the Mohideen Restaurant the other day, hoping that some advice was forthcoming from them. Unknown to him, she was shuttling back and forth between her parents' house, planting in their minds the seed of dislike and hatred towards him with fabricated stories that were difficult for any sensible and prudent person to believe.

Ashman visited Ashfah's parents and related to them and after a lengthy explanation he rested his case. He was then served mee rebus with earl greys tea, it ended with an assurance from them that they would do their best in reaching an amicable settlement.

"Why would Ashfah go the extra mile in pushing for a separation?" said her father, who'd just retired from the police force and was about to settle into civilian life. Her father was known to be a no-nonsense officer and a gentleman who was the pride of the local community.

Soon after, in one of her routine visits to her parents' house, her dad told her to sit down and discuss what she was up to. After giving another pack of lies to discredit and tarnish the image of her hubby, she was stopped in her tracks by her dad.

"I have listened to enough of your tales, and I don't buy most of them. I find Ashman to be a model husband who didn't go clubbing. There are no stories of him being a womaniser or a gambler, and he doesn't even drink or smoke."

You are the one who was unfaithful to him, and he was steadfast about it, hoping you would repent to Allah and take a new leaf from there. I didn't find anything flawed with him, except he might not have the money to shower you with all the jewellery that you wanted."

On hearing that, Ashfah was speechless for a while and shed some crocodile tears, with the hope of drawing sympathy from her mum and dad. As it was to be, she returned home empty-handed, but she was very determined to get her wishes, come what may. She was also warned by her dad not to poison the mind of Ashley, who was now in her teens. As an estranged wife, she'd shown no remorse at all since the fateful night. Her confidante and lawyer, Yati Mansur, continued to expedite the separation proceedings despite her dad's strong advice. She had already paid Yati five thousand just to open up a file for separation proceeding; such was the fee for the most notorious female Syariah lawyer in town.

After a couple of weeks, Yati called her to ask for further instructions, and her reply was, "Give me a little time to calm my dad, because I need some blessings from him."

Yati told her, "I am a busy lawyer, and at this point I have time to attend to you. Otherwise, you may have to wait a little longer."

By now Ashfah discovered that Yati was a mean and aggressive character who would drive her clients crazy. It seemed that money was the only order of the day.

Following that, Ashfah called up her so-called trusted friends for further advice. As it turned out, she had more bad friends than good ones, and this shaped the way her decision was going to be. Shortly after that, she had a dream that she was reunited in heaven with Ashman. As the Malay superstition goes, such dreams occur when one didn't wash the feet before going to bed.

Her elder sister, Amelia, whom she was avoiding along during her strained relationship to Ashman, suddenly came into the picture with the same advice as her parents. Amelia was staying in Malacca with her husband, and she was comforting Ashfah during this period while other vultures in the form of opportunistic men lurked around her, waiting for any slip-ups. Ashfah, as stewardess material, was tall and lanky at five feet seven with a BMI of twenty-five. To men on the street, she was stunningly beautiful and devastatingly attractive.

Amelia came to PJ for one of the weekends and stayed at her parents' place. There, they discussed the matter more profoundly. Dad in his smoking pipe did a watching brief on behalf of Ashman and Ashley. This was the closest that their family got together, with malice towards none. Then came a phone call from Yati asking for instructions.

"I'll give a decision next week," replied Ashfah in a toned-down manner, because she was at the crossroads of her matrimonial life and needed some rethinking of her impending move.

Meanwhile, Ashman was prepared for the worse. Should a writ of summons come from her lawyers, he would be prepared. On one instance at home, she told him, "Don't be surprised one of these days if a policeman comes and handcuff you." Brushing off those ill-mannered comments and warnings, he remained quiet and didn't say a word.

Sensing this threat that came from her, he kept thinking about what next steps she would take. Without further delay, he contacted his lawyer friend on his next course of action. After some consultation from his lawyer friend, he decided to prepare himself.

The following day, he was introduced to the legal firm Azrin Lee & Co. One of the lawyers by the name of Mohamed Chan Abdullah was called upon. Mohamed Chan, a Muslim convert, was a Syariah lawyer registered with the Muslim Lawyers Association. He was practising Syariah Law and knew well his counterpart, Yati, who would be acting on Ashfah's behalf.

Ashfah made a final decision to go ahead for separation. Though this was expected from her, it was she who forced the others around her to respect her decision, because it was her future and her own life. This news reached Ashman through Ashley, and on hearing that decision, he was calm and composed. On the other hand, Ashfah was not calm or composed. Before the legal proceedings commenced, she made a rather bold decision to move out from Ashman's house and seek refuge in her parents' house. The question that remained was Ashley and whom she would follow. Ashley finally made up her mind to follow her mum, not wanting to be alone in the house when her dad was in the office or on trips. Ashman reluctantly agreed to release her to stay with her mum.

A couple of days later, the writ of summons reached Ashman, sealed and delivered by Pos Laju Malaysia from Yati & Co. On receipt of this, he handed the summons to Mohamed Chan without much delay. The stage was now set, and their matrimonial problems would end in an unlikely setting of the Syariah court at Shah Alam, Selangor. After twelve and a half years of marriage, they were to discover that marriage was not a bed of roses – no thanks to the real estate business and Noorudeen, whose proliferation in wheeling and dealing with Ashfah culminated in the couple's marriage being on the rocks.

Upon discussion with Mohamed Chan, it was revealed that the writ stated that Ashfah wanted a talak, or Muslim divorce, from Ashman under section 47 of the Islamic Enactment of Selangor, which stated that either party could file an application asking for a first-degree divorce if both parties agreed, in which case the Syariah court could grant the divorce. On his instructions, Mohamed Chan responded officially to the writ, and the legal proceeding followed suit at a date and time that was to be set by the Syariah court. While waiting for the court appearance, Ashman was told by his lawyer that Yati contacted him and had a friendly chat with him on the matter. The gist of their conversation was that should he refuse to grant the divorce under section 47, she would proceed further under section 50 and ultimately section 53, where the Syariah judge would finally grant the divorce after a lengthy proceeding.

Ashman needed some soul searching in the wee hours of the morning as he performed the Solat Istiqorah, or special prayers, for some enlightenment on which direction to take. He did it in a few sessions until he could see the guiding light. As it turned out, it would be in the best interests to release her. It was one tough decision, and his only thought was on Ashley. As the only child, he would lose his custody of her unless it could be proven that Ashfah was an unfit mother. The battle for custody could take some time, and by then

Ashley would reach eighteen years of age and could decide for herself. For Ashman, it might be not much of a problem because she was staying within the vicinity, and his visitation rights would not be a problem.

The hearing began one fine Wednesday at the lower Syariah court, and both parties were present. Act one, scene one was about to begin, but the Syariah lower court judge postponed the case for the day because he had to attend to urgent matters. Both parties returned home empty-handed. The next hearing was another month away, and this time the presiding judge took the seat and hearing. All concerned parties were in the court room, waiting for their cases to be heard.

In an hour it was Ashfah Abu Bakar versus Ashman Mohamed Ali, and the courtroom was half filled. Not wanting to spill the beans or wash dirty linen in public, he reluctantly agreed to grant a number one divorce to Ashfah. (Muslims are allowed up to divorce number three, and subsequently reconciliation would have the woman to marry another man, consummate the marriage, and then get a divorce before remarrying the former husband.)

The certificate for divorce took about four weeks to be ready, which was common in the bureaucratic machinery of the Religious Department, but that didn't matter much to Ashfah because it was her greatest wish since that fateful night of 28 June to be free from him. To her, all the years of unsettled matrimonial matters had been laid to rest, and she desired for a new man in her life. Any other matters to her took a back seat. Nothing could describe the joy of her victory over Ashman.

Chapter 6

A Moment in Time

Was Ashman fated in this manner to lead a miserable life after the split? Far from it – he was a much stronger person than ever before, although Ashfah thought he wilted under pressure. Some of his unfriendly colleagues who were prophets of doom were quick to ridicule him. Instead, this separation gave him the energy to be forceful with added vigour, and he discovered his true potential. It was like playing football with ten men: one may be a little bit handicapped, but the extra drive and determination made a cutting edge. Ashman did what he had to do, though a tough decision was executed. As he sat on his rocking chair and closed his eyes, memories of the good old days still lingered in his memory, and he cherished those wonderful times. But history took its own course. Time would heal most wounds, if not all. Life had to go on, with no exception. Ashfah had a sky-high ego and told her close friends that she'd won the "personal battle"' with him.

Meanwhile, Ashman took a short break from work and decided to take a trip to the Cameron Highlands by train from KL to Tapah Road, with a few friends. Upon reaching Tapah Road, another friend from his Liverpool days was waiting for them, and they went up the hill station to enjoy the cool temperatures. The hill station still had buildings left over from the English era, like the Lakeside Hotel with its Tudor architecture, similar to the one in the Lake District. A few nights' stay at the hill station was sufficient to freshen him up, and no one talked about his break-up. They took the time to relax in the serene environment.

It was a memorable trip, and the group visited the tea plantation. In the afternoon after lunch, they enjoyed boating at the lake, and they had an evening tea in the town of Tanah Rata. Night meant good, hot dishes for dinner and a trip to a karaoke centre. At the local markets, strawberries were in abundance, and with yogurt they made a wonderful starter for any meal. During the stay, Ashley called him to make him comfortable, and she told him to get some strawberries to bring back to PJ.

Back in PJ after the short trip to the hill station, he delivered the fresh strawberries to Ashley and some souvenirs to his former in-laws. Life went on as usual to him. Two months had passed, and it was time for him to visit Kota Bharu to savour some local delicacies, like ayam perchik, grilled chicken with a coconut milk topping and gravy. His close relatives asked him of his separation and advised him to be strong and preserve. One of them asked whether a replacement was on his mind, and he answered, "Not for the time being." Others interpreted that to mean a reconciliation could be possible in the edah, or cooling-off period, which was around four lunar calendar months.

As the dust settled, there was another startling development. Now that edah, or the cooling period, was over, there was no chance of reconciliation without marriage solemnisation. Ashfah was not at all interested, and it was reported that there was a new man – or men – in her life during that cooling-off period. As mentioned earlier, there were vultures circling around her, and all of a sudden the evil and insidious Noorudeen appeared from nowhere. There was competition from others once a woman becomes free from marriage bonds. As the story goes, con man Noorudeen told her,

"I was in South Africa for a while, working on a project. In between I had short trips to Transylvania, and now I am back here for short while." This time around, she learned not to trust him.

Meanwhile, Ashley's hopes of a reconciliation without another marriage solemnisation between her parents were dented as the cooling period ended. She was frustrated over her mum's attitude and scorned almost every man who tried to court her mum. Her grannies had an open mind by now, even though Ashley was very protective of her mum. As days went by, she took time to be with her dad, who managed to console and comfort her. Ashman managed to find time to be with his only child, and father and daughter got together for some social and leisure activities, including attending wedding invitations in the Kelang Valley and other towns in the peninsula. By now Ashley had grown up to be a full teenager, and her pastimes and IQ reflected that she had come of age.

Back in the office, Ashman was again busy working on the newly secured railway projects. He was able get a few assistants under him, but he needed to travel north for inspection and reporting. His project team was involved in the construction of the present ETS train service from Kuala Lumpur to Butterworth, though this project was not in the same league as the TGV or Shinkanzen. Nevertheless, Malaysians would hail this fast-speed train as a measure of achievement for the country. His schedules initially were quite hectic with meetings, but he still found time to be with his daughter.

On weekends he was always at home with Ashley. The office learnt that he was separated from Ashfah, and gossip spread like fire, though he tried to keep it discreet so that only close friends knew about it. During the company's annual dinner and open day, most of them noticed the absence of Ashfah. Some whispered,

"Why didn't he bring Ashfah along? I had noticed that a few times before".

Others, especially the young and single ladies, said, "I think Ashman is single again. I heard that he is a single father now."

Whatever brickbats he received, Ashman stood steady in the light of office gossip, which was a common feature of Malaysian daily life. One day his immediate superior called him to have a friendly chat and to brief them on the latest development of the project. A little digression on some personal matters prompted Ashman to let the cat out of the bag. At the office, Ashman was never short of secret admirers from the ladies, who were attracted by his simple ways and down-to-earth approach; others were attracted by his friendly appearance and his ability to converse in English extremely well, courtesy of his Liverpool student days. Those were the hallmarks of his characteristics, which also gained him entry into United Engineering Berhad.

Over at the Syariah court, the matter was still not over yet. Ashfah filed a substantial claim for harta sa pencarian, or joint income, over the property and chattel under Ashman's name. This was apart from the mutaah, or allowance for her during the cooling-off period. This time the proceeding would be heard at the Syariah High Court because the claims exceed one hundred thousand. Again the claims were made through Yati Mansur. This time Ashman stuck with his lawyer, Mohamed Chan, and they took substantial time and leaves from the office to attend to the claims she made. What an astonishing figure made by Ashfah, wanting to claim half of the value of the bungalow house left by his late father and other monetary claims.

After a series of court hearings, both lawyers sat down and worked out something for their respective clients. He was advised by his lawyer that court hearings were sometimes postponed for various reasons. He learned that it could take up to thirty-six months to be settled if Ashfah were adamant about reaching an amicable settlement. Some horse trading between the lawyers was necessary, as well as convincing their clients accordingly. Legal fees could reach twenty thousand, depending on the time required.

Ashman was doing some calculations over his own legal fees and how he intended to raise such a big amount – and of course another huge amount for the joint income claims. He thought of selling the house while there was still no caveat from her, in order to raise the money; at the same time, he could look for a smaller house and move to a different locality. Those were the options open to him, or he might raise a loan to cover those claims and fees. This time he sought advice from his cousin in Shah Alam to manage the financial situation. A few pieces of advice were given, and another set of options were available. Borrowing money from relatives was ruled out.

In one of the hearings Ashman attended, the judge asked him, "Do you agree to settle this matter out of court?"

He replied, "Yes, Your Honour, I intend to do so."

The proceeding was adjourned to allow both lawyers time to discuss and then inform to the court of the decision. After much discussion and persuasion, Ashfah finally agreed to the compromise. Though the amount agreed was not a whopping figure, it burned a hole in Ashman's pocket, and he had to cough up the money for the legal costs.

Ashfah also wanted the matter to be settled soon. After fifteen months of deliberations, and her wedding bells were soon to be heard again. Ashman couldn't believe his eyes that she would tie the marital knot again because she used to tease him in an arrogant manner, "Man cannot live without a woman after divorce, but a woman can!"

Ashman's savings from various portfolios, including the Pilgrimage Fund Board, was just enough to pay for the settlement. His savings were enough for him to perform the haj when his turn came, in a couple of years. Now he had to wait because the savings needed to be replenished. To his mind, it was an irony that his separation with Ashfah, who was his childhood friend and neighbour, was created by an unqualified engineer in the real estate business. He sometimes lamented,

"What wrong did I do to deserve all this? Is it Allah's way of testing me?"

With those words, he felt that patience rather than laughter was the best medicine. His payment to her to cover the alimony and joint income settlement was sent through

Mohamed Chan, who held it in trust until the court order was obtained.

The whirlwind romance of Ashman and Ashfah ended in the unlikeliest of places, in the Syariah court of Shah Alam. That era was unlikely to be the same for him again. In today's world of the fast track, one has to adapt to changes to keep abreast with the times. He said, "Let bygones be bygones," and he was now prepared to start a new lease on life with vigour and without Ashfah, who had been a thorn in his side for quite some time. High hopes and spirits dominated him as he searched for a new woman in his life. By now he was determined to make sure success beckoned him. A famous quote from a well-known local scholar and chief minister, the late Tuan Guru Nik Abdul Aziz, read, "One should not be bitten by the same snake that comes out from the same hole twice."

In the interim, Ashman had now more time for hiss leisure activities, like music and football. Ashman Mohamed Ali, as his full name suggested, had been eager to meet his namesake in the form of an English football player and manager, Alan Ashman. The latter brought the English FA Cup to West Bromwich Albion in 1968 and the League Cup runners up in 1970. Then the team WBA had a prolific striker in Jeff Astle, who went on to represent England in the 1970 World Cup in Mexico. Other names on the team were John Osborne and John Talbot. After reading some literature on the club, he became interested in meeting his namesake.

The name Ashman was picked by his grandfather, but it was mere coincident that both had the same name. Ash didn't meet him in England during his Liverpool days, but after reading his biography, he had an admiration for this man who was successful in his short stint at the Midlands club, and who'd worked with mostly average players and a small budget, unlike the present-day English Premier League's top teams. Prior to that, Ash had studied some literature on the former WBA manager, picking up the finer points on the success of the man. He wanted to travel back to England to meet his namesake at a later date, to exchange ideas on football. But before he had time to take a break to revisit England, he learnt that Alan Ashman had recently passed away. The meeting of Ashman and Ashman never got off the ground.

Chapter 7

In Quest of the New Mrs Ashman

"The journey of a thousand miles starts with a single step."

Ashman remembered well the famous quote from Confucius as he gradually charted his future. His passion for music continued after the separation; indeed, it was one of the ways that he was able to compose himself aside from the daily prayers. One evening he was listening to the song called "Spanish Harlem" by Cliff Richard. The lyrics read, "There's a rose in Spanish Harlem, a real red rose in Spanish Harlem." Then he thought of an English proverb that says, "A rose by any name would smell as sweet." There were many roses within his circles, waiting to be plucked.

One day an old friend called him on his cell phone. He'd last met her six months ago after a decade of absence, when they'd first met at Old Trafford Stadium in Manchester. Her name was Faridah Kamar, and she was from Teluk Intan, Perak. She worked in Putrajaya's government offices. She made the first move, and in the initial encounter she looked warm and friendly. But as time passed, her true colours were displayed. She was more obsessed with her work and was financially independent. She was elusive and evasive at times, so it was touch and go because it didn't go the way he wanted. He decided it should end there.

A second encounter wasn't anything worth mentioning, but he now felt that he needed to find a woman in his life after Ashfah had left him in the lurch. There were many admirers both within his circle of friends and through social media. He would prefer to take a step-by-step approach rather than rushing into another relationship. There was nothing for him to rush into, anyway. He kept thinking, "If the mountain doesn't come to Muhammad, then Muhammad will go to the mountain."

Gone were the days of his first marriage to Ashfah, who was practically delivered to him on a silver platter.

There was a lady he met through a friend named Halimah Hassan, who was a single mother and homemaker with two grown-up children who lived in Shah Alam. It didn't matter to him about getting a single mother as a replacement, as long as there was some sort of chemistry between them. Halimah, who drove a Mercedes, had a pleasant disposition and was charming.

They were seeing each other for a while. They began to reciprocate house visits, and she would prepare something for him for weekend lunches. It was then the Aidil Adha Raya and she prepared the dishes for the Raya festival, and he went to her place and brought back what was prepared. Following that, they met at the gazebo of Subang Jaya to watch World Cup football on the big screen while having a simple dinner. She developed some interest in football. Halimah liked the way Ashman carried himself, and they tried to understand more of each other.

Apart being a homemaker, she was also involved in a little direct selling and the money market as well. She made some money from the money market when times were good, but she knew the timing to get out temporarily if the market was stagnant or sliding down. She was a simple and unassuming lady. Her charm was that she was comfortable with anyone due to her direct approach to life. She wanted to travel back to Alor Star and was ready to introduce him to her family, but Ashman wasn't ready yet and needed more time for the courtship in order to understand her better. From there it started to slide down in their relationship. They developed a strain in their relationship that did not improve as the days went by. In the end, the courtship did not last long. Matters had gone awry – or was it Halimah's way of testing him? Only she would know the answer.

In the end, they decided that the best way was to break up and find their own ways. Ashman pondered on the break up with Halimah. "Is it a blessing in disguise?" Again he had the feeling that "If at first you don't succeed, try again". Feeling a bit relieved, he quipped, "If I pursue the relationship, it could end up similar to Ashfah." It was back to the drawing board again for Ashman. Even Ashley understood the matter when he confided to her, and she was now able to hold her own.

One fine day, Ashman he was leaving his office, another of his colleagues came up to him to have coffee at the office cafeteria. Alex Tan, his colleague from the human resource department, started the subject matter and indicated that one lady in her late thirties was still single and available. Ashman laughed at the suggestion and told him, "You know I would not want to date anyone from the office."

Alex Tan was astonished and asked again, "But why?"

"If matters goes haywire in our relationship, the whole office would know, and I do not want to be the centre of gossip. It could go even up to Tan Sri," answered Ashman.

"Give it a chance, and God willing, if it works out, you'll be all right," said Alex Tan.

That kept Ashman thinking about it. Who was this mysterious lady was on his mind.

The following day, Alex Tan turned up again in the evening. By now Ashman was ready to say yes, and the name mentioned was Nur Nilam Sari, a human resource clerical support staff who hailed from Perak.

"Perak again!"

Ashman exclaimed. Alex Tan told him to relax and not be so prejudiced. "Okay. What have I got to lose?

"Again Alex Tan told him to relax, and Alex would talk to her in order to pave the way.

They did not want other office colleagues to know, so Alex Tan told him that their first meeting would be in Jakarta, in order to avoid prying eyes that would lead to gossip. Ashman booked a KLM flight package including hotel and transfers, plus a welcoming Nasi Padang dinner on arrival. The scheduled flight was from KL to Jakarta the following week on Friday evening, and the return was on Monday morning. He had to take leave on Monday. The plan was that she would be chaperoned by her close friend from Alliance Bank, Wan Suria, during the trip, and they'd share a room in Jakarta Hilton. "Why Jakarta?" asked Ashman.

Her reply was, "Nur Nilam wanted to buy some nice Indonesian kebaya that would cost one hundred per set."

Ashman got the message that he might have to pay for it, but it was no harm to him because he was prepared for those shopping items. In order to purchase the tickets, Wan Suria, whom Ashman treated as the runner, supplied him the details of their passports.

Come Thursday, Nur Nilam Sari texted Wan Suria over the cell phone and dropped a bombshell by informing her that she was not be able to make the trip. Both were flabbergasted. Wan Suria and Ashman were speechless at the response from her. Her text read, "No need to trouble yourself by sending me the tickets."

He could not comprehend the action taken by Nur Nilam and why she'd chickened out in the eleventh hour. She was the one who'd set the terms and conditions of their first meeting. Ashman had spent over three thousand for the trip, and not only had the money gone down the drain, but he was also made to feel embarrassed. He asked Wan Suria over the phone, "Am I being taken for a ride?"

Trying to calm down Ashman, Wan Suria said, "I will talk to her again."

On Monday, Ashman decided to confront Nur Nilam at the office. He set foot in the human resource department, but to his surprise, she was on leave. This was the most frustrating time for him after being jilted by Ashfah, and he could not contain his disappointment. Two days later, he went to her office, but she had given him the slip. He wrote a note and placed it on her table at her workstation: "I would like to meet up with you ASAP." The next day, he called her over the office phone and told her to meet him at the office cafeteria at four in the afternoon. This time she turned up, not wanting to create a scene at her office. Over the coffee break, there was nothing more to say other than the grandfather stories and fairy tales of yesteryears. At the end of the coffee break, he told her,

"Very well, then."

Ashman was soon to learn that Nur Nilam had an uncanny knack for giving surprises, and she could keep others guessing and waiting at bay. Perhaps the previous bad experiences reflected on her current behaviour and characteristics, but Ashman thought the best for him was to keep some distance. Being in the same building might not be that easy, and sometimes they'd bump into each other. One day they met on a company's Aidil Fitri Raya open house at Kuala Lumpur Equestrian Club, at Bukit Kiara. It could not be avoided that both of them had to be in a group photograph together with the managing director. Ashman brought Ashley to the occasion. Nur Nilam saw Ashley and confided to Wan Suria that Ashley had some semblance of Nur Nilam during her younger days. But the similarities ended there, and were no further follow-ups.

Back home, Ashley asked him, "Why was that lady staring at me?"

His answer was, "I don't know. Might be you reminded her of someone she knew."

On another occasion, Nur Nilam tried to make amends for her indifference by offering to sell him some steamed fruit cakes that were home-made by her friend. Of course he always had good intentions, and he was prepared to purchase a few boxes at thirty each. They proved to be yummy. Fruit cake was one of his favourites, and Ashley loved them too. A few orders were made, and he could only consume one box; the rest were charitably given to the nearby mosque during the Thursday night prayers. Initially, it was no more than a commercial transaction. After a couple of weeks, he ordered more due to requests from the mosque, and it became his routine to bring those yummy fruit cakes to the mosque on Thursday night while others sponsored the dinner.

In September, he learnt that Nur Nilam's birthday was around the corner. Not to be left alone while his buddies were wishing her a happy birthday, Ashman bought her a new cell phone to be presented as a gift. As usual, while delivering those cakes to his car, he thanked her and paid the money. Then he took out the box containing the phone, though it was not gift-wrapped. He gave it to her and said, "This is for you as your birthday present."

She reluctantly received it and told him, "I hope there are no strings attached."

In turn he joked, "You didn't see any string there. Anyway, there are no strings attached; it's just a token because the other day I was unbecoming to you."

She smiled, thanked him again, and walked back to her office. Unknown to him that was the last of the orders because her friend no longer baked those cakes.

As matters worked out, there was a lunch treat by Ashman to a young trainee at the human resource department. He offered to buy lunch, and on the request of the trainee, she would like him to invite a few more office colleagues rather than be seen just the two of them. Coincidentally, Nur Nilam's name was mentioned because she was sitting next to her in the department, as well as another person named Linda, who was their immediate superior. "Not a problem," he said, and so it was a lunch provided in honour of the trainee at the nearby Secret Recipe Restaurant.

Ashman came early and booked a table for four. When the three of them arrived, Linda sat opposite him, and the trainee sat next to her. There was only one seat left, was next to him, for Nur Nilam. Nur Nilam took that seat but moved the chair a little bit farther away so that she was not too close for comfort. Her body language was well read by Ashman.

In December, another year was about to pass without any signs of that new angel from paradise for Ashman. By now he'd had a few hiccups in his encounter with a few of the ladies. He realised that there was no straight path towards rebuilding a new life, and the ladies that came by didn't measure up to his expectations. By now he had known more than half a dozen of them, but none of them were worthy of being mentioned. He quipped,

"No wonder they are unmarried or single mothers." His search continued, and that ushered him into the New Year.

Chapter 8

Ashman Meets Azmah

Social media had become a powerful tool for human interactions, and it transcends national barriers. Upon realising the potential of it, Ashman indulged himself with Facebook. He started on a small scale, and in one year he garnered ninety friends, mostly made up of close friends, relatives, and office colleagues. When time permitted, he opened up Facebook, but only at home. His office hours were strictly for the company's purposes because he was a man of high integrity.

One of his office colleagues, Rosalinda Jaafar, was his friend on Facebook, and she was quite active then. One day the name Azmah Abdul Aziz appeared as a friend to her. That enabled him to add her name as a friend request, and within a couple of days the request was accepted.

He thanked her for accepting him as a friend and started the ball rolling on messages, plus a number of likes on her postings. There was also another friend within Azmah's circles, by the name of Zaharah Mahmood, who was an Australian PR but had her roots in Subang Jaya. It took a while before he was acquainted with Azmah through Zaharah, who gave him a helping hand. He shared many interests with Zaharah, and music was a common factor. He uploaded for her a few songs that were not available on YouTube. Zaharah was delighted with that, and the friendship prospered.

One fine day, Zaharah was posting the latest photo of her and her daughter in front of the famous JM Beriani Restaurant in Subang Jaya. Ashman asked her. "When did you come back to Subang Jaya? You should let me know, because I want to give you a lunch treat, especially at that restaurant."

Her reply was, "Hehe. Next time around."

Not satisfied with the answered, he told her, "When are you flying back to Perth?"

Her reply was, "Tomorrow afternoon. Actually, I was here four days ago."

Ashman told her that he would catch up with her.

When she was back in her home in Mandurrah, Perth, Ashman contacted her again, and Zaharah told him,

"I have a phone number for Azmah in case you want to speak to her in person."

What a pleasant surprise for him that he obtained more than he'd asked for, and he was indeed indebted to her. He began to message her over Facebook, informing her he got her cell number from Zaharah and asking whether it would be all right to contact her when the need arose. To his pleasant surprise, there was a favourable response from Azmah, and she said he could call her.

Before calling her, he went through her background on Facebook and discovered some information about her. She was a homemaker in her middle forties with two grown-up boys, but her husband was suffering from some disorder, and much of her of time was spent tending to her hubby. Ashman thought there was no harm in getting more acquainted with her, and he found her to be a warm, demure person.

She was from Batu Bahat and attended Temenggong Ibrahim Girls School. When she completed her studies, she worked as a flight stewardess with Malaysia Airlines because she had the height and built of one. Complying with the requirements of being a stewardess, she was warm, friendly, affable, and affectionate. She left the job upon marrying her hubby, who at the time was double her age.

One day he decided to call her over the phone, and his first words were, "Hi, Azmah, this is Ashman."

"Oh, hello there. What a pleasant surprise to have you calling me."

He continued. "Hope I am not taking too much of your time. My own rule is that it should not be more than fifteen minutes."

"As you wish, but I am quite free now."

The rest of the conversation was getting to know each other. Ashman was the one to end the conversation, and he wished her a good day and well wishes. Before hanging up, he asked her, "Shall I call you Az?"

Her reply was, "Yes, you may."

The first telephone call ended on a positive note, and that spurred him to greater heights and to follow up.

Getting to know each other for the first time was an exhilarating experience for him as he further looked into her background on Facebook. He learnt through the conversation that she and her family resided at Kota Damanasra, Section 5, another residential enclave between Kuala Lumpur and Petaling Jaya. She had earlier stayed in Johor Bahru, when her hubby was still in the government service prior to his retirement. What intrigued him was her gentle manner and the warm, affable manner she displayed during the conversation.

After the first conversation, he texted Zaharah and again thanked her for helping him to break the ice.

"The rest is up to you," she replied via text. She also told him that Azmah had a good circle of friends that could be of interest to him.

"Okay, madam, I will explore further," was his reply. That was assuring enough for him to proceed.

There was another friend named Anne from Johor Bahru who was also in her circle of friends. Anne was on the verge of separation from her hubby. One day Anne called him to seek some advice about divorce matters. It was a lengthy conversation with her, and Ashman briefed her on all the steps towards separation, including time involved, estimated costs, and the implications thereafter.

Anne had an inferiority complex compared to her peers, who were always on the frontline, and Azmah used to console her that beauty was in the eyes of the beholder. By now Anne was much relieved by a series of advice from him, and she thanked him a lot. She was able to find her own footing and was looking forward to what her next steps would be. Word spread within Azmah's circles that Ashman could be regarded as a "marriage consultant". In a brief jab, he told them, "I'm just a greenhorn in this field."

The second telephone conversation between Ashman and Azmah lasted more than twenty minutes because he did not want to incur much of her time as a homemaker. "Hello, Az. I hope I do not take much of your time," he started.

Her reply was, "Hi, Ash. No, you are not taking too much time, because I am quite free now. A little conversation does not bother me. Anyway, it's been a while since you called me."

"I am glad that I called you at the right time." To continue the conversation, he asked, "What manner of woman are you, madam?"

Her reply was, "I am a homemaker. Are you comfortable if I ask you how long you have being a single father?"

He said, "Well, I have been in the wilderness close to four years."

She had known more of him and his family, and she thought it would be a good idea to introduce another friend to him. She'd known this lady for more than a year through Facebook, but she'd never met her in person.

Ashman received the idea of Azmah introducing her to another lady with an open mind. To him, it would be a pleasure to get to know some of them as casual friends. There was this lady named Zaini Harun from Kangar, Perlis, who was a single mother with two grown-up children studying in London, courtesy of the boys' father financing them. She would occasionally travel to London three or four times a year to meet her boys. She maintained her Kangar house and came to Kuala Lumpur prior to her flight for London. He asked her, "When would I be able to meet this friend of yours?"

She told him, "As soon as possible. I will inform you of the date and time." He thanked her for being so kind to arrange the meeting.

In a fortnight, the meeting was set up for Ashman to meet Zaini through Azmah. Azmah called Ashman and said that she would be coming from Kangar and would put her up at her place before leaving for London the following day.

"I have a pleasant surprise for you: she'll be here earlier than expected," she told him. "Where would you want to meet us?"

Ashman replied, "That's good. I think we could meet at the PJ Hilton coffee house at 4 p.m. tomorrow. How does that sound to you?"

"Great. We shall meet there."

Zaini arrived at her Kota Damansara house and stayed the night there, but they didn't go to bed till two in the morning because both of them caught up with each other. The following morning, Azmah provided him with Zaini's cell phone number in case they needed to contact or locate them upon arrival at the rendezvous.

Ashman kept himself free on that Saturday to meet the lovely ladies at the Paya Serai coffee house at PJ Hilton. A reservation was made for a table of three. He was punctual as usual and arrived at 3.45 to wait at the table. After ten minutes, he spotted Zaini alone, walking towards the coffee house. He recognised her through her photo on Facebook. He walked towards her as she entered the coffee house and greeted her. "Hello, madam. You must be Zaini Harun."

Her reply was, "Hi, Ashman. Yes, I am. In fact, I did notice you while you were at the table."

They shook hands, and he showed her a seat at the table. He asked, "Where is Azmah?"

"I'd better wait for her here because she is still in the ladies' room, doing some touch-ups."

"Very well. We might as well wait for her here," said Ashman.

In a short while, Azmah was seen walking towards them in a catwalk style, which caught Ashman's attention. He had an eye for details. "Hello, Azmah. Nice to meet you," he said as they shook hands.

"Sorry to keep both of you waiting," she said.

Ashman replied, "Don't mention it. We are all glad to meet among ourselves."

It was the first meeting of the three at the entrance of the coffee house, and Ashman ushered the two lovely ladies to the reserved table. On the way to the table, they were met with prying eyes from the men at the other tables, but the trio kept their cool.

This time Ashman did not lay any ground rules as he'd previously done. Zaini sat with Azmah opposite Ashman, and they ordered coffee and pastries. Ashman insisted that there was a high tea buffet, but both ladies wanted to maintain their figures and declined. There was no specific agenda on this meeting of friends from various backgrounds, and the discussion was casual and down to earth. They talked about general matters to start with and touched a little bit on contemporary politics; there was laughter too. Though he was sitting opposite Zaini, with whom he was to be interacting, his eyes were initially focussed on her. As it turned out, Zaini was more of a friendly chat.

As it went past half an hour, Ashman found out that Zaini was more casual and wasn't ready to delve into her life. It could be that this was their first meeting, or it didn't click for her to move forward. Now Ashman had to swing the conversation to Azmah, who was wearing a blue blouse and matching pants. He made an effort to get to know her better. His eyes were more towards Azmah, who was frank and friendly.

To begin with, Azmah told him that she was tending to her hubby, who was already in the early seventies and had some complications not worth mentioning here. "I am just sharing my problems with you. It's not to be construed as anything like running away from my responsibilities. I'm not betraying him in any manner."

It suited Ashman well because he was always listening with empathy and would lend his ears in situations like these.

"I am sorry to hear that," he said. "I am pretty sure you are a patient and humble wife for being able to handle this situation all the while."

Those words of wisdom from him made her more relaxed, and she continued to relate her experience. He said, "Every cloud has a silver lining. If you believe at the end of the rainbow there is a pot of gold, then in order to have the rainbow, we have to withstand the rain."

On hearing that, there was another round of laughter. He then told Azmah that he was impressed by her for being able to take all this in stride.

Azmah was taken aback by the way Ashman approached the subject matter. She thanked him for the advice to her. Ashman then assured her that she could call him at her convenience if she ever wanted some words of advice. If ever there was another man whom she could lean on other than her hubby, Ashman fit the bill.

The rest of the afternoon was spent exchanging views on bringing up their children. When Ashman showed Azmah his family photo, she told him that Ashley more resembled her mum, and Azmah showed him her two boys were still studying in upper secondary school. Zaini didn't show any photos of her children. It was now six o'clock, and Azmah indicated that they had to go. Ashman settled the bill. Whilst waiting for the bill, Ashman requested a photo be taken with the three of them, and the waiter was summoned to snap it from the cell phone camera. There were two snaps taken with Ashman seated and the lovely ladies standing behind him. Ashman then relayed the photo to Azmah and Zaini via his cell phone, with the words,

"If we do meet again, why, we shall smile. If not why then this parting was well made."

Azmah was impressed by the above quotes from Shakespeare, and she was also impressed by the impeccable manners and etiquette from Ashman. He assured the two ladies that he would not post it on Facebook; it was for remembrance only. Before saying goodbye, Ashman asked her if they could meet again tomorrow morning for coffee at Amcorp Mall before Zaini's flight in the evening. What a pleasant surprise that she agreed to the invitation. They walked to their respective cars parked at the basement of the hotel, and Ashman saw them off after a successful meeting.

Chapter 9

You'll Never Walk Alone

As agreed upon, the trio met again for morning coffee at Amcorp Mall, a shopping mall nearby PJ Hilton. The place was called Ka Fei Dian, a kopitiam or coffee station situated on the ground floor known for its toast, bread, and coffee. The time set was nine o'clock, and as usual Ashman was there early to book a table. The ladies arrived a couple of minutes later, and Ashman welcomed them to the table. All of them had toast with butter and egg jam, plus coffee. While waiting for the food to be served, the ladies related what they did after the meeting yesterday. Azmah was able to sleep well, but Zaini took a little adjusting to the new place. They certainly slept soundly because they were tired after going to bed late the night before.

Ashman then asked them, "Any sweet dreams worth sharing?"

After some thoughts, Azmah replied, "There was, but I can't remember now."

"It's okay; I was just pulling your leg."

After morning coffee, Azmah said she wanted to walk around the mall because the shops were beginning to open. The trio walked together, but Ashman walked behind them. They were still at the ground floor when Azmah stopped at a boutique to check out their latest arrivals. After looking through the newly arrived dresses, she found one that was of interest to her and asked a shop assistant to try it out. It was a blue modern kebaya with sequins around the neck, and she tried out a medium size in the fitting room. Her slim figure really suited her, and she walked out of the fitting room and showed it to Zaini, who was equally enthralled and said,

"Really gorgeous, Az."

Ashman commented, "Isn't it a low cut?"

Azmah replied, "It's okay for me." She then asked him to take a photo of her with the new dress on, which was dark blue. Ashman took his cell phone camera and snapped it twice before sending it to her. "Wow, look at it. I like it," she said.

She then asked the shop assistant to wrap it for her, and she asked for some discounts. After getting 10 per cent discount, before she reached for her purse, Ashman had already signed his Visa and insisted that he would pay for it.

"No, no, Ash. Let me pay for my dress."

He told Azmah, "It's my pleasure, as a thank-you for all your help." He then looked at Zaini and said,

"Pick up one for yourself, and I'll be pleased to settle it as a gift to you."

Zaini didn't fancy any of those and told him, "Thanks for the offer. Perhaps next time we meet."

With that, they walked out of the shop and went down to the lower ground level, where most of the flea markets were operating. After walking around for an hour, they decided to part company. Before bidding farewell, Azmah thanked him for the dress and said, "Please feel free to call me."

"Okay, thank you, and you're welcome," was the reply. They shook hands and waved at each other with the hope of meeting again.

Back home in the afternoon, Ashman thought more of Azmah and wondered whether upon meeting her, it was love at the first sight. He had not expected such warmth in her to capture his heart, even though she was married woman. Could it be Cinta Terlarang, or forbidden love, for him to be attracted to her? The warmth that she exuded was something that had been missing from his life for quite some time. Did he fall for her, and should he proceed with this relationship? Those were the questions that troubled his mind as he looked for an answer.

The next night, he had a dream. He remembered Azmah was tending to her ailing hubby, and if her hubby were to ascend to the celestial abode, then she would be eligible to remarry. But would he want to wait? And for how long would he have to wait? Those were matters that needed serious attention. After he did some soul searching, he remembered a saying: "Nothing ventured, nothing gained." So with his in mind, he would have to take some calculated risks, but with a Plan B on hand. He did some prayers on this, but so far nothing came out of it. His heart said to go ahead.

Inspired by the theme song of Liverpool FC, Ashman began to tune in to the song while in his armchair, relaxing.

"When you walk through the storm,
Hold your head up high,
Don't be afraid of the dark.
At the end of the storm,
There is a golden sky,

And the sweet silver song.
Walk on to the rain,
Though your dreams be tossed and thrown.
Walk on, walk on,
With hope in your heart".

He downloaded that song to his cell phone and sent it to Azmah with the hope she got the message. Upon receipt of the song, she texted him, "Thank you so much for such a wonderful song. I didn't know that you are such a sentimental person."

He responded, "You are welcome."

Even if Azmah took the song as being strong in the face of adversity, it didn't matter. He wanted the relationship to continue and flourish. In between, he made "likes" and simple comments on her Facebook page, and that did the job of continuing the relationship.

Further texts and photos were relayed to her, and slowly but surely it developed into some kind of friendly relationship. For a moment Azmah didn't think of anything beyond that; she simply focused on her sick hubby.

One day he spotted her at the Jaya Supermarket doing some grocery shopping, and at once he approached her.

"What brings you here?"

She was surprised to see him and answered, "Hi, Ash. What a coincidence! I was just doing my grocery shopping."

He said, "Come, let's have a drink at Starbucks."

They went to the coffee station. This time she made sure she paid for the drinks to reciprocate Ashman's treat the other day.

Azmah was doing more of the talking, and he lent his ears to her and listened with empathy about what was going on with her since they'd last met three weeks ago.

"Oh, I had more to do than I could manage, and my hubby's condition has not improved. At times he showed signs of deterioration, and of late he is sensitive to what has been advised to him."

After hearing all of that, he said, "Be more patient. Anyone in that condition would be equally sensitive."

Those words were music to her ears, and she was now more relaxed and calm. "I wish I had more time with you," she said.

Ashman was glad and answered, "Yes, we can always find time. Otherwise, phone calls will do."

They spent almost an hour at the coffee station before she excused herself. As before, she said to him, "I'll call ya."

Ashman was elated with that meeting and looked forward to meeting her when the time was right.

The next day he went to office as usual with high spirits. His colleague Alex Tan noticed some changes in him and said, "You must have hit cloud nine, Ashman. Share with me, if you don't mind."

His reply was, "Well, nothing much, except ..."

"Except what? Tell me."

"It's not about Nur Nilam Sari, but I met this one person, a homemaker who was friendly to me."

Alex's instant reaction was,

"Ha! Better be careful – could be another Poison Ivy."

Ash was startled on hearing that and related half the story to Alex, who soon understood his situation now and told him,

"Be careful. You could be walking on thin ice." Not wanting to prolong the discussion, they both went off to attend to their respective meetings.

Ashman was packing his office items to go home after a long day's work. His cell phone rang, and to his surprise it was Azmah on the other line.

"Hi, Azmah. It's a pleasant surprise for you to call me."

She wanted him to know that she was thankful for him and the advice he'd offered to her yesterday.

"How nice if we could have dinner together," he jokingly told her.

Her reply was, "Not so soon, dear. Give me some time because I have a lot of constraints." It was a better answer than Ashman had expected.

One day, Ashman noticed Azmah was at the same location for grocery shopping, and she was about to walk to her car. Ashman greeted her, and while walking to their cars, he asked her, "Now that I know your father's name, Abdul Aziz Mustafa, would you mind telling me your mother's name?"

In a low tone she told him, "Rahimah Abdul Rahman."

Ashman added, "Oh, now I see why your name is Azmah, which is combination of your father's and mother's names."

She exclaimed. "Hey, I didn't know that. And all the while, my parents didn't tell me that!"

"I am just guessing. If it happens to be true, what a coincidence!"

"Thank you, Ashman. You really made my day. When I am back home, I shall ask them."

Ashman accompanied her to the basement car park of the building, and while walking, he casually told her,

"If only we could work out something between ourselves, life would be different."

Without asking him for further clarification, Azmah got the message embodied in those words, but she remained silent and nodded as an acknowledgement. After reaching her motorcar, she got in, shook hands with him, and waved.

"Bye, Ash. Hope to see you again."

"Bye Az, thank you for your time and we shall meet again" was his reply.

Ashman felt cheerful as he went to his car and headed back home, singing the song "You'll Never Walk Alone" until he reached home. By now he figured that he was making some headway with Azmah in his relationship.

Chapter 10

The Limited Company of Ash and Az

Like acorns that grew into mighty oaks, Ashman developed his feelings for Azmah. Those feelings gradually blossomed into deep love because she was a worthy successor to Ashfah. His continued relationship with Azmah was more than a friend because of the warm response from her was enough to capture his heart. For her, he was just a friend, though she treated him as more of an elder brother as she confided a lot things to him, and he was able to listen with empathy and offer sound advice.

As the days went by, their communication became more frequent. By now Azmah had realised that she might be overstepping her limits, but she was assured that "Friendship Remained and Never End", just like the old acronym for FRANCE. Ashman had to be careful as to when to call her, and he would text her prior to calling. Azmah soon realised that she was impressed and spellbound by Ashman's eloquent way of speaking in Queens's English instead of Manglish, or Malaysian English. That was a head start for their relationship and proved to be a watershed in their romantic journey ahead.

One day, Ashley asked Ashman whether he was seeing another woman. His answer was in the affirmative, but he didn't reveal her identity because it was too early. She understood the situation and didn't want to know further. As it stood, Ashman would like it to be discreet, and he managed to keep it that way. Once or twice a week, he would call her; at other times he'd text her or message her through Facebook. His yearning to meet her couldn't be underestimated because it remained an enigma to him, but patience had been a blessing for him. On the other side, Azmah had develop an inclination for him, and he noticed it.

One afternoon, he managed to get her on the line and spoke for about ten minutes. He asked her, "How are you today?"

Her reply was, "Not too good."

"Cheer up, and let me sing a song for you."

"Okay, what song?"

"How about 'Yesterday'?"

She was puzzled. "Yesterday?"

He told her, "Yes, the song from the Beatles." She was excited as he sang it.

"Yesterday, all my troubles were far away,

Now it's here to stay.

Oh, I believe in yesterday

Suddenly I am not half the man I used to be."

She was impressed by his singing and said, "I didn't know you can sing well."

"I had some vocal training before, and I used to sing at our company's functions." He was trying to be modest. Then he added,

"You too could improve your voice with some vocal training. There is a shop at Amcorp Mall called the Singing Shop for these purposes."

"Oh, really? That's good," was her reply, and she was delighted by the way he approached any subject matter.

He then said, "If I may ask, would you like to go for a karaoke session in the near future? I know of a good outlet."

"I'd love to, but as you know, I am tied up at the moment." Ashman told her, "I think I have an idea. It would be much easier for you to come along with Zaini during an afternoon, rather than an evening outing."

Azmah answered, "Yes. I will let you know once Zaini is in town."

The following week, Zaini was in town and stayed with Azmah. Azmah sought her hubby's permission to go for a karaoke session with Zaini the next afternoon. Permission was granted, and she informed Ashman of her availability. On hearing that, he booked a room at the Neway Karaoke in Subang Jaya. It was a Tuesday, so he had to take a half day from the office to meet the ladies. The time set was 3–5 p.m., and all of them turned up.

Ashman was the first to arrive and was ready to receive the two of them at the lobby. Upon meeting them, he ushered them to the booked room. It wasn't peak hours, so he managed to obtain discounts, and before the session started, they ordered a few drinks and food. He then asked the ladies, "What kind of songs would you like to start with?"

"Hmm. Why not start with soft music, and later duets?" said Azmah.

He selected the evergreens, starting with "Widuri", a popular hit by Indonesian singer Bob Tutupoli. It was Zaini who took up the microphone first to show her singing prowess, followed by Azmah, who did a rendition of "Yesterday". There was applause after the rendition by

Azmah. Now it was the time for Ashman to croon a few numbers, and he started very well with the hit song "Those Were the Days", a popular number by Mary Hopkins. He followed that with "Ferry Cross the Mersey", a hit from Gerry and the Pacemakers. As it turned out, most of initial songs were from Liverpool city. Zaini realised that, and now it was Ashman's turn to relate to them his experiences in the Merseyside and all the moments of joy and glory, especially when Liverpool FC was the most successful team of that era. As they went on, a few numbers were selected, and it was time for duet songs, mostly in Malay. Azmah and Zaini started with a song from ABBA, "Chiquitita". This was followed by the duet song "Sa Iring dan Sa Jalan", another popular number from the late Broery Marantika and Sharifah Aini, by Azmah and Ashman. To end the session Azmah was given the honour to croon the last song which she chose an evergreen song by Linda Scott, entitled "This is My Prayer." It was a scintillating performance by her which would herald them into many later karaoke sessions.

At the end of the session, as the trio walked back to their cars, Ashman asked Azmah, "When shall we meet again?"

Her reply was, "Are you serious?" He nodded his head and this prompted her to ask,

"Why?"

"I will speak to you later, when the time is opportune." There was a moment of silence between them, and as Azmah reached for her car, Ashman thanked both of them for finding time for meeting up. With that, they dispersed with all the sweet memories of the afternoon session.

After a couple of days, he decided to call her to gauge her response from the words uttered at the karaoke centre. There was no response from his two Whatsapp questions, so he decided to try again the following day. This time he got the green light to call her, and his first words to her were, "Hi Az. Just wanted to say hello."

"Hi. You were quiet the couple of days. I guess you were busy with your work."

He said, "How on earth would you know that?"

Her reply was, "I think by now I am able to read you!" She laughed."

Yes, it's true, and that is why I called you. I hope everything is all right with you," he replied.

"Not really. My household chores and tending to my hubby has taken a toll on me," she hold him.

"I understand that. No wonder you didn't response to my text yesterday." After a short silence between them, he told her once again to take matters as they went, and they ended their conversation.

In this kind of situation, Ashman had limited access to her and kept thinking it might not be easy to meet her often. Then he had an idea, and during one of his conversations, he suggested that both families meet for coffee or breakfast, bringing along their children without them knowing why. She told him, "Hey, that's a good idea. You bring Ashley along, and I'll bring my two boys, Amri and Amran. Where shall it be, and when?"

His reply was, "Shall we meet this Sunday for dim sum at nine in the morning?"

"Where is the venue?"

"We'll meet up at the Chinese restaurant at Quality Hotel, Kuala Lumpur."

Permission was granted by her hubby for her to bring the two children; of course her hubby would like to stay back in the house on a Sunday morning, and she promised to be back before noon. The meeting was set, and they brought their children along, who had no idea what was it about. As usual Ashman and Ashley arrived before the scheduled time and sat in the far corner of the Chinese restaurant, which was on the second floor of the hotel. Then Azmah came with her two boys aged seventeen and nineteen, and they sat at the middle table. Not all the tables were full at that time, and both sides were able to look at each other, but the parents pretended not to know each other.

For the first time, Ashman was able to see in person her two grown-up boys, and she saw Ashley. Though both of the parents met at the buffet table to take their food, they behaved as if nothing had happened. Ashley was quick to notice the two boys but had no inkling of what was planned by their parents. After an hour, Ashman was leaving the restaurant, and both parents settled their respective bills. He then asked Ashley,

"How was the food?"

She said, "Good. We should come here more often."

Ashman nodded as he got a glimpse of Azmah and her children. As it went, the meeting between them was successful, but what next?

In the evening, he texted her and thanked her for being together for the dim sum session. He insisted that he should have picked up the bill. She told him,

"That's okay. Give me a chance to settle my own."

Back at the office on Monday, he was again in high spirits after meeting her, when his next outing with her would be was always lingering on his mind. He had to think of ways to be able to meet up with her. This limited company and time was not what he wanted, but he had to make do for the time being. Zaini was slowly drifting out of the picture; her occasional appearances were only to assist Azmah and draw her out. Azmah was not too comfortable with this clandestine relationship, and she sometimes wished that Ashman would slow down his pace.

In order for him to proceed in this relationship, Ashman thought that he would have to meet her to convey his feelings towards her and make known to her his plans and how they would possibly materialise. Having a candlelit dinner would not be possible at the moment unless she was accompanied by Zaini, and to him, three was a crowd. It was also difficult for her to be out in the evening alone other than grocery shopping because it might create suspicions by her hubby. They had to be discreet about it.

Ashman did not have much choice over this, so he planned to have a high tea with her on a weekday. He carefully selected the day, place, and time to meet her. He had to take a half day leave, and he asked her, "How about meeting up for high tea at Holiday Villa in Subang Jaya?"

She replied, "Anything special this time?"

His answer was, "Yes. I've got a surprise."

"You know I don't like surprises."

But he was quick to make her comfortable by saying, "It's just a cup of tea, and maybe we can talk anything that comes to our minds. It's been three weeks since we last met."

With that assurance, she agreed to the invitation and allowed him to fix the time.

As usual, he arrived early and waited for her at the lobby of the hotel. After ten minutes she arrived, and he ushered her to the Palm Terrace Coffee House. At the coffee house they selected the high tea buffet, and the Pasembor was one of the popular dishes. Drinks flowed as usual, and after waiting for some time, she asked, "What is it that you wanted to say?"

"Relax, my dear. I think by now you have realised that we have been seeing each other more often, and quite discreetly too."

"Yes, I realised that."

Ashman told her of his feelings towards her and added, "It's been difficult for me to drag out this meeting and relationship for too long without coming to a decision. I long to meet you all the time, but at the moment, you are still tied up. In any case, if you are available by default, I would like to go further and ask for your hand."

On hearing that, she was startled for a moment. After a couple of minutes, she said,

"I understand your feelings, but at the moment I am unable to commit to anything."

"I wish to apologise if you are offended by that, but is it all right for the time being? I would wait for the time to come, if you could accommodate me some space inside your warm heart."

"My dear Ash, you have to be a patient man. When the availability comes by default, I would be glad to consider your request. But before that, I might have to gauge my two boys' reactions to this."

"Okay, that will be fine to me. But you need to be cautious on this matter."

She said, "Don't worry. I'll take your advice, and I will consult you in whatever steps that I take."

The high tea session ended on a positive note on both sides, and he walked her back to the car, which was valet parked at the entrance.

Would time be of the essence to Ashman? This was what was bothering him at times, and the availability for him to meet her was limited, so he could not throw caution to the wind. Every step had to be carefully examined because a wrong foot would ruin whatever relationship that had been built upon to this day. Up to this stage, he had maintained manners and etiquette, and he only shook hands with her only. Never had it crossed his mind to take advantage of her, but their relationship was extraordinary.

Chapter 11

The Buyout Clause

Ashman reckoned that he had registered his interests with Azmah for the first option available for him, should she be free from any encumbrances. He likened that to be an "invitation to an offer" by the legal language, or more recently the principle of a buyout clause in football circles. If Azmah's hubby were to ascend to the celestial abode, then she would be able to marry again after her edah, or mourning period of four months and ten days. This is the Muslim way of matrimonial matters when a widow was allowed to remarry but was still subject to wali, or guardian, consent. Unless an agreement was not reached, the Syariah law would take its own course. Discreetly or otherwise, he had registered his interests in her.

Why did he have to register interests in asking for her hand before she was eligible to remarry? Most of his close friends would ask that, and his answer was that in many Asian societies, marriage by match-making parents was still prevalent; this was even true for a widow or female divorcee. As a lady of beauty, grace, and warmth, Azmah would never be short of admirers and suitors. This fact was recognised by Ashman, who felt that he needed some proactive action to secure the bid. In Muslim marriages, there were no buyout clauses, but there were practices for some high-powered men to pay a fee to the husband for divorcing his wife; though not common, it happened. Such was the current scenario in Malaysia.

Ashman thought that was the best move at the moment, which was to register his interest in her. That was clearly understood by Azmah, who shared the same feelings. They maintained their discreet relationship and would only meet when it was necessary; otherwise, their contact was only through cell phones. Even Ashley didn't know this arrangement and was relying on her dad to update her.

One day Ashley asked him, "How long are you going to remain like this, Dad?"

He replied, "I really don't know. God willing, I hope it will not be too long."

One day he called upon his Syariah lawyer, Mohamed Chan, and fixed an appointment at his office to discuss matters over the so-called buyout clause. The following day, he stopped at the office in Kelana Jaya and greeted him. "Hello, Chan. I am here to trouble you a bit and discuss in a casual manner."

Chan said, "Sit down, and let's have some coffee." He asked his tea lady to prepare coffee for them in the meeting room of his small but cosy office. Before the discussion, they exchanged notes on the current political development and football, though Mohamed Chan was an Arsenal fan.

After twenty minutes, Ash opened up the subject matter, and Mohamed Chan was stunned by his ideas and proposed offers to Azmah. "I've never heard of this before, but it is a worthwhile proposal."

Ash explained to him that he had clandestine meet-ups with her and wanted Chan to provide the necessary advice.

Before that, Chan told him to recall the normal marriage vows: "To obey and to honour, in health and in sickness, till death do us part."

Those magic words were what Ash needed, because the death of a husband would render the women eligible. He added, "If you are willing to wait, that would the necessary course of action."

"At the moment, I am willing to wait for a while."

According to Chan, in Muslim marriages there were few qualifications on the above words, and a divorce could still occur by default, which was currently practised when before solemnisation of marriage the imam put the following conditions:

1. When a man leaves his wife without giving her financial support for four consecutive months or more, without trace or reasons. If she files a complaint to the Religious Department with Ringgit Malaysia 1.00 and it's found to be true, then the first divorce occurs.

2. When a man does bodily harm to his wife, and she files a complaint to the same department, and upon investigation it's found correct, then a first divorce also takes place.

3. When a man voluntarily utters the words "I divorce you" to his wife, either in film, on stage, or any other circumstances, then it is also a first divorce, unless he is insane at the point of utterance.

As advised by Chan those were the circumstances that made divorce by default. There were no specific buyout clauses in Muslim marriages, but if those were to be construed as a buyout, then it was a matter of opinion.

"What about those provocations that could lead to any of the above situations? Could it be invoked as a divorce by default?" Ash asked.

"Yes, it could, if the authorities are satisfied that there is a prima facie case." He further cautioned him that those cases could take some time.

Ash asked, "Chan, how about the wives whose husbands are paid handsomely by some high-powered people to divorce them so that they can marry them?"

The answer from Chan was, "If the procedures were correct, then it becomes legal even though the intentions were questionable and immoral. But we leave that to Allah to judge."

Ashman nodded and said, "Power and money tends to corrupt." The last option was never on his mind. In the end, he told Chan as he was about to leave his office.

"Thanks for your legal advice. Now I have a clear mind."

Ashman pondered over the matter. To him, the best option was to wait for Azmah and when she would be available by default – not that he wished her hubby would die. Would he be willing to wait, or would he set a time limit and look for other options. Soon after dinner and a cup of hot milk before going to bed, he set his alarm to wake up at two in the morning. In the wee hours of the morning, he woke up, took his ablution, and conducted a soul-searching special prayer to get some enlightenment from Allah. Sometimes enlightenment didn't come immediately but through consistent prayers and over a period of him. This spurred him to make it a routine.

Chapter 12

An Indian Summer

It was now mid-year for the loving couple, and they met each other in one of the pre-haj courses at the Tabung Haji Complex Hall in Kelana Jaya, which was some kilometres away from both their houses. Ashman was scheduled to perform the haj this season, and Azmah was more or less confirmed because she'd registered a long time ago. He'd only registered four years ago, and in order to expedite his turn, he had to purchase the premium Tabung Haji package instead of the normal Muassasah system. She also took the premium package system for more convenience. As a rule, she had be accompanied by her hubby, a guardian, or what was referred to as muhrim, any of the Tabung Haji's authorised male personnel.

This time her hubby would not accompany her not only due to ill health, but also because he had already performed the haj solo, more than ten years ago. Every Sunday morning, the course was conducted at the Tabung Haji hall, or surau, for the intended pilgrims. This was also a golden opportunity for Ashman to meet Azmah, albeit for a short while during coffee breaks. In the second session, she brought him a home-cooked lasagne and told him,

"This lasagne was cooked early this morning, and I'd like you to have it because I know you love it."

He said, "Oh, that's great. Now you know what my favourites are. Has anyone asked you why you are baking this and bringing it to the course?"

"Oh, I usually do it for my friends at this course, but I leave some of it at home for them."

In the weeks that followed, they met during the coffee breaks, and Ashman would arrive early to meet her prior to the commencement of the course. Sometimes they would discuss or revisit the lessons and exchange notes. He bought her some literature on the haj, which was sold at the bookstall at the ground floor. On one occasion she brought him some lamb beriani rice from home, which was an Arab speciality. He asked why she'd brought home-cooked Arab food this time. Her answer was,

"I learnt this from my mother, who had some Arab blood, and this was one that I mastered."

"Oh, thank you. I didn't know that. Now you will be going back to your ancestral land," he joked.

"I am impressed by your culinary skills." After he tasted the rice, they were off to the classroom for further lessons.

The difficult part was to bid farewell to each other once the sessions were over. Towards the end of the pre-haj course, they had to do some practical programmes like the "stoning the devil" ritual, which had to be at night at the Tabung Haji complex. Participants were offered to rent the rooms at the hostel within the complex, though some would spend the night doing some prayers at the hall without catching forty winks. Azmah wanted to sleep over at the hostel with other Muslimat, or female friends, but Ash would do some prayers at the hall and catch forty winks after the rehearsal was over.

It was on a Saturday night, and the rehearsal started at nine o'clock after dinner. Everyone was in their ihram, or the haj costume, and with such a large number of participants, he had difficulty identifying her. He called her over the cell phone, and after meeting her, he said,

"My, my. You look different but great in the ihram costume."

She answered, "Oh, thank you. Let's head to the hall for the briefing."

After the briefing, there was a break for refreshments, and again he looked for her at the canteen as promised. Upon locating her, he said,

Let's find a table for us to quench our thirst. The temperature for the night is still warm." They managed to find at table at the corner, shared by other participants.

She took out what was prepared from home and told him, "This what I prepared for you: roast lamb. I know you'll like it."

Without hesitation he told her,

"What a kind-hearted lady you are. I didn't expect something like this tonight. You must have been busy in the afternoon! Thank you once again, and I am certainly proud to have you."

"Oh, stop it. I know what you're gonna say. Anyway, you're welcome."

He then said, "I am sorry, dear, but you seem to be able to read my mind."

"It's not that, but a woman has a sixth sense." Without further delay, they savoured the dish and some drinks to go with it.

The programme was a success. Everyone performed the rituals correctly, which went in the wee hours of the morning. It ended well before the Suboh prayers, but Ashman was able to catch some sleep before muezzin's call for the prayers. After prayers, they had some coffee, and Azmah told him that she needed to rush home. He offered to escort her home to Kota Damansara by trailing her car to her destination. This was the first time Ashman had seen her house, and he drove way to avoid creating any suspicion.

Back at home, he took a short morning nap. He was soon back on his feet again to head for Amcorp Mall for the Sunday flea market. After lunch with Ashley at the mall, he was back home again. He thought that his first step of securing a buyout clause was completed, and he thought about what his next moves were. By now she was able to comprehend the big picture, and time was of the essence. Now he had to wait for a while. His focus was on the intended pilgrimage to the Holy Land. The same was true for Azmah, and whatever discussions from now on were to on that subject. There were twenty weeks of brief encounters or meetings between them, like an Indian summer, and both cherished it. To Ashman, it was like an opening to a new dimension in his life.

Chapter 13

A Pilgrimage Extraordinary

It was now the haj season after the Aidil Fitri Raya and in the year 2013. Both were busy after the Raya celebrations. Azmah was the first to receive the good news about confirmation for her intended pilgrimage from Tabung Haji or the Government Pilgrimage Board. Ashman was still waiting for the offer since he'd made a late application. On receipt of the confirmation, she called him to break the good news.

"Hi, Ash. I finally made it, and my flight KT 29, which is an early slot for the haj."

He answered, "That's good news for me. I hope to receive mine as early as possible so that I can make the necessary arrangements with my visa and medical check-up."

"Don't worry dear, I want you to know that last night I dreamt that you would be getting your call very soon." Those words provided some relief to him.

The next couple of days proved be uneasy as Ash waited for the news from Tabung Haji. In this instance, no news was not good news. It was on a Thursday evening after the Magrib prayers that he received a phone call from Tabung Haji: his intended pilgrimage was confirmed, and he was asked to bring his passport for the preparation of the haj visa.

He was slotted on flight KT 95, which was towards the end. He was delighted and immediately texted her to relay the good news. She was the first to know before any other family members, and within minutes she texted him back.

"Congratulations! I am glad to hear that."

With that, Ashman informed his family, close relatives, and friends.

The following day, he managed to get her on the line to exchange information about their preparations so far. Now it was Azmah who had mixed feeling about the haj trip. Her mind was also on her sick hubby: should anything untoward happening, she might not be there for him. Even though the planned arrangement of their boys and relatives to take care of her hubby during her absence was made well in advance, she still had some fear. Her hubby had consented to her going solo, and his prayers for her had been a source of encouragement.

Ashman told her, "We have done our part and seek and pray to Allah for the best."

Those comforting words from him renewed her with vigour and eagerness for her intended pilgrimage.

Later in the day, Ashman proceeded to the Tabung Haji for his haj visa arrangements and to collect his medical check-up booklet. After collecting the medical booklet, he went to an authorised clinic for a comprehensive medical check-up, including the mandatory meningitis injection. As arranged earlier with Azmah, he would meet her at the government clinic in Kelana Jaya for the check-ups. After two weeks of not seeing each other, they met at the government clinic. While waiting for their turns, there was time for catching up with each other.

She told him that she intended to have a thanksgiving dinner for all relatives and friends in a couple of days at her house. She added,

"I am afraid I can't invite you as yet."

He replied, "Understood. That reminds me to have one, once the paperwork is done. Maybe I will have to go back to my hometown to meet all concerned before the trip."

Her preparations were almost complete, except for tying up loose ends. His prep was at the beginning. During that period, they were in communication with each other, and he would learn from her as he manage those initial preparations almost single-handedly; later his relatives and Ashley helped him. He told her,

"How nice if we were to be together now, making all the preparations."

She answered, "Be patient, dear. This is a test of our patience in the near future."

With those consoling words from her, Ashman felt on top of the world, and his excitement for performing the haj could not be described. It was a dream come true for both of them.

Azmah's departure for the Haj was scheduled on flight KT29 in early October, which would take her to Medinah prior to arriving in Makkah for the pilgrimage. Ashman's flight was now confirmed for KT95, which would take him direct to Makkah some twenty days later. There was an excitement for the pilgrimage as the day drew near. When preparations were ready for her, the following evening was to be her flight from KLIA, Sepang. As usual the check-in was scheduled to be 10 p.m. at the Tabung Haji Complex at Kelana Jaya, the same venue as the pilgrimage course. Azmah was accompanied by her two boys, her hubby (using a walking stick), other relatives, and close friends. Ashman was there too and was mingling in the huge crowd to see her off, unknown to her family. Earlier in the morning, she'd texted him of her departure plans, and they hoped to have a glance of each other. As the crowd waved goodbye to the pilgrims, Ashman was there among her relatives to do the same. He saw that she wore a black jubah, or robe, on departure day.

She arrived in Medinah after a nine-hour flight, and upon checking at the Best Western, he was the first to be informed via a Whatsapp message from her cell phone: she'd landed safely and was resting in the room. He replied with zeal and enthusiasm, hoping to meet her in Makkah later. They were scheduled to be placed at the Zam Zam Tower Hotel, opposite the Grand Mosque of Masjidil Haram. During her eight-day stay, he called her a few times, and at other times he texted her. In his first conversation he said,

"Try to pray as much as possible at the Prophet's Mausoleum, seeking forgiveness to the Almighty, and ask for our union to be a reality."

She replied, "Yes, I will."

He added that the Warriors Cemetery at Jabbal Uhud was another place to pray and recite prayers, seeking solace and requesting one's needs.

Next was the journey to Makkah for the haj requirements, and to perform certain rituals for her and the group. After checking in at the hotel, she spoke to Ash again and informed that everything went well for her. Ashman was delighted to hear that, and his flight was scheduled in another eleven days. He was looking forward to meeting Azmah over there.

Ashman was soon to board his flight at Tabung Haji, Kelana Jaya. He had a surprise and saw an old flame, Faridah Kamar, who was also sending off her relatives. However, that did not deter him from his focus to send off Azmah and to perform the haj.

Ashman was accompanied by Ashley and his close relatives and friends. He wore an ihram costume like the rest of the male pilgrims. The huge crowd like the one during Azmah's departure didn't make him anxious, and he entered the departure hall and waved goodbye to all. Invariably memories lingered about seeing Azmah with a few tears. He vividly remembered Azmah wearing a black robe two weeks ago, waving towards him.

Flight KT95 arrived safely and on time at the Jeddah International Airport, but baggage handling and the immigration process took more than three hours. Immediately upon arrival, he texted her, and she responded well, expecting him at the same hotel in the later part of the afternoon. It was almost dark when he checked in at the hotel, and she had already gone for the Magrib prayers at the Grand Mosque. Upon completion of the check-in, he had to rush to perform the Tawaf ritual with the rest of his group, and that took him past midnight with no chance of seeing her that evening.

The following morning, Ashman met Azmah at the coffee house at the hotel after Subuh prayers. It was their first meeting since the send-off at Tabung Haji in Kelana Jaya. His first words to her were,

"Az, I am delightful to meet you again. How are you doing so far?"

She said, "Thank God, I am doing well, and Allah has answered my prayers to be fit and to perform the haj without any difficulties."

"I am extremely delighted to hear that. I hope we both are able to do the same."

They completed their breakfast meeting. As planned, they were to visit Jabal Rahmah in the next two days, so they went down the lobby to register their names for the visit to the Tabung Haji package counter. The journey to Jabal Rahmah, which was near Padang Arafah, would be the grand meeting place of all intended pilgrims, and it would take half an hour by chartered bus.

Ashman and Azmah were ready for the visit, and she wore white pants for ease of climbing the hill, as well as white gloves in case he wanted to hold her hand and assist her to climb with her ablution still intact. The visit to Jabal Rahmah went as schedule, and soon after breakfast, they boarded the bus together with some thirty other intended pilgrims. The bus reached the destination in less than twenty-five minutes because the traffic was clear.

Upon arrival, they alighted from the bus. From the bus parking to the foot of the hill was some thirty metres, and both of them walk side by side for the first time towards the foot of the hill. The height of the hill was less than five hundred feet, but the path was a little bit treacherous, and they needed to be extremely careful. This Jabal Rahmah, or hill, was the very one when Adam met Eve after descending from heaven to earth. It was still the symbol of eternal love, and most Muslims asked for prayers to be united with their loved ones, or for divine intervention on such matters. On arrival on the foot of the hill, he said,

"Can you manage yourself on this slippery surface, or may I help you by holding your hand?"

Her reply was, "Yes, please, you may."

"Just stick with me, and we'll walk slowly to the top. If you want to stop halfway, let me know."

The ascension to Jabal Rahmah started very slowly for both of them, with Ashman leading the way, holding her hand, and guiding her step by step. At midway they stopped for ten minutes to catch a breather, and they sat on a stone as they watched other climbers determined to get to the top. Inspired by others, they continued the journey at a much slower pace, to be careful. The sun was beginning to rise, and the heat was high, but the climbers were undeterred by it. Both of them were sweating a bit but continued the climb.

At last they reached the top and offered special prayers, asking for divine intervention for them to be united someday and make their paths merge without much hindrance.

After another fifteen minutes, they conquered Jabal Rahmah as both of them reached the peak. They could not stay for too long because the place was congested. After saying their wishes and prayers, Ashman looked deep into her eyes and asked her one question.

"Azmah, will you marry me someday?"

There was silence on her part, but she nodded her head.

"Yes, dear. When the time is right."

"Great! I will take care of you more, from now on."

She then cautioned,

"It won't be smooth sailing – you have to be patient."

With both of them exchanging promises and vows, they smiled at each other and walked down the hill. By now they discovered that the rear of the hill had concrete steps leading down. He held her hand to descend step by step with high hopes that their prayers would answered in the near future.

Once they reached the foot of the hill, they headed for the bus that was waiting for them. The other climbers were already inside the bus, and so they were the last ones to board. Ashman still found time to give a few riyals to children asking for some donation, and she bought a Hijrah calendar from the small children as a little help for those needy people. On the bus, the pilgrims were merrily relating the experiences of climbing Jabal Rahmah. Ashman sat beside her and talked of other matters.

As the bus travelled back, the driver stopped at a small place called Tanaim and informed the group that they could stop and buy refreshments at the nearby shops. Before alighting, Ashman offered the rest of the bus passengers coffee and some snacks, and the bill was on him. Upon hearing that, they gave him applause and said,

"May Allah grant your wishes from the prayers at Jabal Rahmah."

Azmah was coy about it but remained silent, and he ushered her to the restaurant. After the refreshment break, the pilgrims thanked him for the treat.

Back at the hotel, they parted company for a while before preparing to go for Zohor prayers at the Grand Mosque. Though it looked like they had more time for each other, the programmes were tight. During the five daily prayer times, they could walk together to the mosque because he was chaperoning her. At other times, including meals, she had to be seen with the other female pilgrims. He was more than thankful that the stay in the Holy Land was more than he could have asked for.

Before the next haj requirement, which was a trip to Arafah for the Wukuf programme, Ashman brought two prayer mats of the same colour and design at the nearby arcade. He showed her, and she was delighted. He told her,

"I bought the two special prayer mats. They are spongy and able to withstand the hard, rough surfaces over there. At the same time, you can use it for your forty winks."

She replied, "Thank you, my dear. How thoughtful of you."

The peak of the haj was the grand gathering at Arafah for another two days, which was one day before the Raya Aidil Adha. All pilgrims congregated at the Arafah open field to pray and listen to the sermons. Then they performed special prayers to Allah after Asar prayers. This was the highlight of the Wukuf programmes, and in default the haj would be rendered null and void. On that day, they boarded the bus to Arafah, which was a stone's throw from Jabal Rahmah. They arrived in the late evening due to traffic congestion on all roads leading to the Arafah; only Saudi locals could use the direct train services from Makkah to Arafah. Food and accommodation in tents were provided, as well as toilet facilities. It was a night to remember for all intended pilgrims, likened to the Day of Reckoning. It was also one of the spots where prayers would easily be answered, God willing, because the satanic devils were being relegated to the brink of doom in this instance.

Intended pilgrims were put up in separate tents according to gender, except for the VVIP, who paid a premium for more comfort. On reaching Arafah, they split company but met during meal times. She would recite the Koran while awaiting the big event, and the same was true for him. During lunch, when they met, he told her,

"After the Asar payer, I will find a suitable place for us to do the special prayers together, to seek divine intervention for our wishes."

Again she nodded, showing agreement, and it surprised him that she was obedient to him, which was not always the case in her previous marriage.

Soon after, they found a suitable spot. They prayed. After that, he told her, "Let's do the special chants to Allah for half an hour, before we pack our bags to head back."

"Okay, dear. I am with you," she replied. No other words could describe Ashman's joy and relief upon hearing those words from her, as well as her body language. When it was time to depart for Makkah from Arafah, as they'd agreed, he waited for her at the prescribed bus stop. While waiting for the bus, she opened her container of biscuits and dates for him, which she'd brought from the hotel. Again he was delighted and said, "Thank you. How thoughtful of you." He gave her a new bottle of Zam Zam holy water to go with it. Without saying a word, she smiled at him, and it was one of the greatest smiles he had ever seen.

On the bus, the pilgrims were tired. Though they sat next to each other, there was no way he would put his head on her shoulder; strict rules were observed in the Holy Land, and both had high hopes to complete the haj in distinction, or haj mabrur, so that their prayers would be answered by Allah, as well as their repentance being accepted. Traffic was bad and congested, so they arrived at the hotel two hours later, at midnight.

Another programme was awaiting them at Makkah. This time it was the circling the Kaabah or Tawaf seven times, anti-clockwise, while chanting special prayers inside the Grand Mosque. Here they had to part company again because there was a big crowd, and everyone had to take care of oneself so as not to cause a stampede or any untoward incident. After the ritual completed, the last event for the night was the congregation from Safaa to Marwah, which was also inside the Grand Mosque. Before the Tawaf, he told her to wait for him near the entrance to the Saffa with the group. After forty minutes, the Tawaf was completed, and the group members walked towards the entrance of Saffa. From a distance, he could recognise that she was waiting for him, and he quickly approached her with a big smile.

While waiting for further instructions from the group leader from Tabung Haji, they had a rest for about ten minutes. This time Ashman took another bottle of Zam Zam holy water and offered it to her to quench her thirst. "After you," she told him, but he told her he had another bottle. His thought was, this is the first time she's wanted to share the drink from the same bottle. Their affection grew by the day. He insisted,

"Please take a separate bottle, because I do not want you to drink something that could be contaminated with mine."

After much hesitation, she took her own bottle, but he wondered whether she wanted to test him on how much of a gentleman he was. Nevertheless, he was focussed on the next event.

In another five minutes, the congregation from Safaa to Marwah was about to start for the group. This time there were no holding hands for them because each would walk at his or her own pace seven times, or three round trips plus one. At one particular stretch, all were required to do a brisk walk, reminiscent of Prophet Ibrahim's wife, Siti Hajar, walking briskly to fetch water for his son, Ismail, a later prophet. In one of the rounds, she dropped something from her bag, but he was there to pick up for him, risking being run over by others from behind. To him, true love knew no bounds, and he gave the item to her, which was a small box of tissues. She smiled at him in an attempt to thank him. Again he wondered whether she could be testing him, to know whether he'd go the extra mile.

After twenty minutes, the event was completed by the group, and as they dispersed, he walked back to the hotel feeling exhausted. When they reached the hotel, he waved to her because they wanted to retire as soon as possible. The following day would be the Aidil Adha Raya, where all pilgrims would do their sacrifices by slaughtering goats, sheep, cattle, or camels, by paying the relevant bodies to do the work for them. Invariably, all pilgrims would wake up early for the Subuh prayers and perform special prayers for the Raya. Though no special festival came after with the likes of visiting relatives and loved ones, the atmosphere here was more holy in nature.

Ashman and Azmah were ready to go to the Grand Mosque for the Raya prayers, and they were still in the in haj costumes as they greeted each other for the Raya greeting. Off they walked to the Grand Mosque. She told him,

"The spirit and soul of the haj has given me the strength to move on and forget. The usual homesick feeling is not here with me."

He nodded and replied, "That is true devotion to the haj. Let us hope when we go back, we'll be better persons."

She was silent on those magic words that came from him. She loved all the words of wisdom he spoke, especially on occasions like these.

The next haj requirement was the event called "stoning the devil" in a place called Mina, which would commence after midnight. Prior to that, the group collected stones either from Makkah or Mudzdaliffah. Intended pilgrims were required to pass through a place named Mudzdaliffah and, if possible, collect some stones from there. For Ashman and Azmah, who took the Tabung Haji packages, there was an option to commute from Makkah to Mina for two consecutive nights, and the rituals were performed at three main devil's pillars after midnight. At Mina too, both were able to perform special prayers to seek their wishes from Allah. The same prayer mats were used in the special prayers at Mina.

After the event was successfully completed, she told him, "I am glad we have completed the haj requirements without any hitches."

He smiled at her and replied, "Thank God we are able to do it."

Immediately after performing the Suboh prayers, the group boarded the bus back to the hotel, and everyone seemed relieved and satisfied they were able to complete the haj requirements without much hindrance. Azmah was in good health up till now, except for a few moments of headaches. Ashman was all right so far; perhaps her presence had spurred him into greater heights, and it was a tonic that he required and that had been missing from him since his separation from Ashfah.

He asked her, "Now that you have completed the haj requirements, what is your plan now? Go shopping?"

Her reply was modest. "That is a good idea. Would you accompany me?"

Instantly he answered, "Yes, of course. Let me know the time and day. You have completed the haj, but I still need to visit Medinah after your departure to Kuala Lumpur."

Back at the hotel, they had breakfast together while listening to some haj lessons given by their group leader from Tabung Haji. After that, they went back to their respective rooms to catch some sleep because they were awake the night before at Mina. Ashman, who shared his room with two others who'd departed early for Kuala Lumpur, had the room to himself. Azmah still had three other pilgrims to share with. Both of them didn't complain about creature comforts or food because they'd paid a premium for the packages.

That evening, he invited her to have afternoon tea at the famous Felda Café, located at the second floor of the hotel, to savour some Malaysian delicacies. He asked her, "Would you like to have Teh Tarek and Roti Canai down at Felda Café?"

Instantly her answer was, "Oh, thank you, I'd love to. Could you wait for me another ten minutes at the lobby?"

"Aye aye, madam, I shall wait for you."

He waited at the lobby, and upon her arrival, he ushered her to an empty table and sat. As a self-service restaurant, he went to the counter and ordered the food. He then brought to table Teh Tarek, Roti Canai, and some curry to go with it.

She asked him, "Do you remember the last time we had Roti Canai?"

"Yes, when we were attending to a course at the Tabung Haji complex five months ago. But it seems only yesterday."

After some conversation on other matters, they felt relaxed and left to prepare for Magrib prayers without bumping into anyone they knew.

The following day, they found time to do some shopping in the morning. Some of the items sold in Makkah were bargains, especially electronic items and gemstones. They were at the nearby arcade to do some window shopping, and they wandered around to see what was of interest. He then took her to one gemstone and jewellery shop and began looking at the items on display. There was this sapphire gem that was of interest to him. He asked her, "Isn't that sapphire beautiful?"

She replied, "Oh, yes, but if you are thinking of getting it for me, please not at this moment."

"Okay, I understand, but I want to get something for you over here. Just a remembrance of our short stay here." She was silent on that.

After leaving that shop, they sat on a bench outside and exchanged notes on what had happened during their stay in the Holy Land. As usual, she had more stories, and he was a good listener. She told him,

"I got a call from my hubby and the boys yesterday. They've managed well without me."

He said, "That's good. I think you deserve a break to do the haj after all these years of tending to them. Now your prayers are answered."

On hearing, that she gave a smile with a happy but composed mood.

Ashman saw from a distance a watch shop and persuaded her to have a look at the shop. He kept his self-discipline of not holding her hand and observed the "dos and don'ts" with her.

Inside the shop, they examined a wide array of watches for ladies and gents. She was the busier of the two because she had an eye for details. At one stage he noticed that she kept an eye on one of the watches, and he immediately told the shop assistant to take it out from the display for to try it out. She tried it out and looked fascinated by the design of the watch. Without further delay, he told her,

"Would you be kind enough to accept this watch from me as a small gift during haj? If it is not too much to ask?"

Azmah was spellbound by those powerful words. She looked right at him and replied, "I suppose I can't refuse this time."

He nodded and told her,

"I am glad that you have now accepted my offer."

He proceed to the cashier for payment. The watch cost only one thousand, but her acceptance of that was a milestone to him in his effort to win her heart.

By now it was almost eleven, and the couple walked out of the arcade. Ashman noticed there was a Starbucks outlet at the next floor and invited her to have some coffee. She agreed without any hesitation. They sat at one corner of the shop to have their coffee. He asked her,

"When was the last time we had coffee at Starbucks?"

She pondered for a while. "Was it at Amcorp Mall some time ago?"

He was delighted with the answer and told her that her memory was excellent, but more important in his mind was that the chemistry between them. After sipping coffee, she stood up and insisted she settle the bill as a goodwill gesture for the gift that she'd accepted. He nodded and thanked her for the coffee. It was almost noon, and they left the place and headed back to the hotel to prepare for the Zohor prayers.

After the necessary preparations, they met at the lobby. He waited for her to once again chaperone her to the Grand Mosque. Upon reaching the inside of the mosque, she would be with the other ladies of the group, and Ashman went to the men's group for the prayers. After completing the prayers, they would meet at the Babus Salam gate, which was the main gate, and then they'd walk back to the hotel to have lunch. This programme would be repeated the last day for her in another four days, but he still had to visit Medinah before flying back. Anxiety slowly crept into him because he would have to part company with his dearest Azmah. She remained silent when asked about her departure. To her, the magic of Makkah had transformed her into a much better person, and she was grateful to Ashman for being her soul mate and the nearest person to her apart from her hubby.

Anxiety crept in for Ashman. He would be parting company with Azmah because the stay in the Holy Land was almost up, and the business of limited company would start again once they were back home. Filled with sadness, he went to tell her that this was the moment he dreaded most, but he hoped to be reunited as soon as possible, God willing.

In reciprocation she told him,

"Be patient, my dear Ash. For every cloud, there is a silver lining. As you always sing to me with your Liverpool song, we should hold our heads high when we walk through a storm."

He said, "Okay, I will walk on, until we reach our final destination."

They comforted each other in the wake of uncertainties back home. That night he couldn't sleep well, and instead he woke up for special prayers in the wee hours of the morning, to ask for wishes that money couldn't buy.

The moment of truth finally arrived for Azmah: group KT29's departure for Kuala Lumpur was scheduled for tomorrow afternoon. She wasn't able to hold back her emotions on the eve of departure, which was mixed with happiness and sadness. She had happiness for completing the haj without much hindrance, and she felt sadness for parting company with Ashman, whom she regarded as her husband in waiting. "Torn between two lovers" was an apt description.

Even though she had to perform the last ritual of the final Tawaf around the Kaabah inside the Grand Mosque, her facial expression showed feelings of melancholy, and tears dropped from her eyes as she wiped with a handkerchief provided by Ashman, who was with her during the ritual. Upon completion, they walked out from the mosque and waited for the bus to take her and the group to Jeddah for the return flight to Kuala Lumpur.

While waiting for the bus, she said,

"What could be more daunting and dangerous than our relationship, which is built on love and trust?"

He tried to answer that.

"Hmm. For us, ever since the duel between Habil and Kabil, or Abel and Kane, the world has stood still, waiting for what will happen."

These were strong words from him when he was in his element, and that left her to hope for the magic wand from Allah.

The bus arrived, and Azmah was draped in blue jubah, or a robe with white gloves. She bid farewell to Ashman with some tears. She then offered to shake hands with him, and for the first time she kissed his hand as a mark of respect and gratitude to her dearest soul mate and her husband in waiting. It was a touching moment for him because they'd maintained some distance between them. Now it was openly declared,

"Till death do us part."

She was the last passenger to board the bus, and he continued to talk to her until the bus was about to move. His parting words to her were,

"Azmah, I am be proud of you. If any woman were to be put on a pedestal as an example of the pinnacle of a loving and caring wife, you are the one – a man's woman, sweet and charming, cool, calm, and composed. You are the angel of my life!"

There was no flattery in the above words from Ashman and his sincerity was felt deep inside her. In reciprocation, she gave him a sweet smile, and as she waved to him, the bus pulled away slowly before going to full throttle. Ashman continued his haj programmes in her absence.

The following day, when she arrived in Kuala Lumpur, she called him at the airport while waiting for luggage clearance.

"Hello, my dear. I've just arrived at KLIA. Thanks you for your prayers for a safe journey without any hitches."

His instant reply was,

"Thank you, Az. I am glad you have landed, and I shall continue to pray for you. I hope we are able to meet again when I am back there. Take care."

"Bye, Ash. I love you."

For the first time Azmah uttered those words, and they seemed to come out naturally. These were the milestones of their relationship.

She was received by her two sons because her hubby was not feeling too well on the day of her arrival. Soon after, she was back at her Kota Damansara house, where a small thanksgiving dinner was hosted for close relatives.

For Ashman, his haj programme had one last event to complete: make an eight-day visit to Medinah the week after. While in Makkah, he managed to do some shopping and bought prayer mats and other related items, to be presented to relatives and well-wishers back home. He would pack all these and send them by courier, which would take more than ten days to reach and before his arrival home. Occasionally he called Ashley to find out news from home. He continued to text Azmah to keep in touch with her.

The trip to Medinah was set to be on a Thursday. Ashman and his group of pilgrims performed the final Tawaf at the Grand Mosque in the afternoon. The bus took the group on a five-hour journey from Makkah to Medinah with frequent stops at the R&R, and by the time they reached the second holy city, it was almost dawn and time for Suboh prayers. After check-in at the Best Western, he received a message from Azmah that read, "I miss you. Hope you are okay." It was noon in Malaysia, and he felt relieved. As the saying goes, "Absence makes the heart grow fonder."

He texted back, "I miss you too. Lots of love, and take care".

The programme at Medinah was to pray at the Nabawi Mosque forty times in eight days, a visit to the Prophet Muhammad's Mausoleum (which was at the mosque), visits to other neighbouring mosques, and finally a visit to the Warriors Memorial Mausoleum at the foot of Jabal Uhud, where the famous Battle of Uhud took place centuries ago. The Warriors Memorial Mausoleum was another special place apart from the Prophet's Mausoleum as a place for special prayers with high hopes. The visit to the Warriors Mausoleum was on a Thursday, and Ashman made a concerted effort to perform the special prayer just outside the concrete wall, which acted as fencing for the mausoleum. Immediately after the special prayers, he took out a marker pen and wrote on the wall,

"Azmah and Me."

It was not an exaggeration to say that this was a testimony of his love to her, which surpassed that of Shah Jahan and Mumtaz Mahal.

It was time to bid farewell to Medinah and the Holy Land. Ashman's group ended the programme on a high note, and everyone was eager to return to Malaysia and be reunited with their loved ones. Ashman managed to send messages to Azmah, whom he now considered his other half. The return flight to Kuala Lumpur was in the afternoon and scheduled to arrive at KLIA at past midnight the following day. As the aircraft landed at KLIA, he texted her to inform her that he'd arrived safely. A similar thanksgiving would be held at his house the following day.

For Ashman this pilgrimage was one of the highlights in his life, more so in his quest for his angel from paradise which should not be a mirage anymore to him. In Azmah he had found his new love, a love that was conceived at the first sight.

Chapter 14

One Sparrow Does Not Make a Spring

It was business as usual for the loving couple back home in PJ and Kota Damansara. After a couple of days, Ashman was back to the office with wishes from his colleagues for a haj mabrur, or haj with distinction; she received the same wishes. The line of communication between them was by texting and occasionally a phone conversation.

One day she told him that her hubby, Azman Ali, took a turn for the worse. She was in tears, but he manage to appease her, and that was the tonic she needed from him to get back on her feet again. As the days passed, there were no improvements on her hubby's condition, and she was much occupied tending to Azman; she hadn't met up with Ashman since arriving home from the Holy Land. However, Ashman kept giving advice to her to be strong in the face of difficult times, and he continued to pray and hope for the best. He texted her that this could also be another form of test by Allah in order for them to be resilient.

Two days later, she called him to inform that her Azman was taken to Damansara Medical Centre and was admitted to the intensive care unit; he was unconscious. He immediately appeased her and told her to remain calm and recite the small Koran, or Yaasin. She was at the medical centre with her two children, and no visitors were allowed, so there was still no chance of him seeing her.

On the second day of admission, Ash tried to text her whether visitors were allowed, but the answer was in the negative. On the third day, Ashman decide to pay them a visit under the guise of being an old friend. As he was checking at the reception counter, to his surprise he saw her and the two boys accompanying a hospital bed to a waiting ambulance outside the main entrance. Upon checking with the ICU, he was informed that Azman was taken back home at the request of his family, and there was little chance of him surviving. He called her and informed her what he'd seen.

She told him, "That is true. We are bringing Azman home because his last wish is that he wants to be at home for the final hours."

Ashman was moved by it and told her to remain calm and leave it to Allah. He then asked her,

"Is there anything I can do to help?"

"Not really, but I will let you know when I need you."

Ashman continued to recite the Yaasin in his house. The following morning before dawn, he received a call from Azmah that her hubby had passed away in his sleep ten minutes ago. Again, this was received with mixed feelings. He recited the Yaasin for the deceased and received updated news via text. He took the day off from office, which was again on a Thursday, to attend the funeral and try to assist her in whatever way he could. He rushed to her house in Kota Damansara to pay last respects under the guise of an old friend, and he arrived at 10.30 a.m. On arrival, he saw a large crowd and went in to have a closer look, as well as join the group reciting the Yaasin. The programme for burial would be after Zohor prayers in the afternoon, at the nearby mosque. He did chip in five hundred for the funeral expenses by giving it to the eldest son.

Everything was in order, and the special prayers at the mosque began on time. Ash carried the coffin with others from the mosque to the awaiting hearse. The journey from the mosque to the burial grounds in Bukit Kiara was twenty minutes, and he followed the mourners by car. Then he saw her dressed in a black jubah robe with her two sons. He stayed a distance from her; up till now, he wasn't being able to talk to her, only send condolences via text. At one juncture, she managed to get a glimpse on him, and she gave a short smile. That smile was enough for him to feel wanted on this occasion. The burial took place quickly, and after the sermons were read, the burial was over. Ashman managed to approach her and say, "Please accept my sincere condolences at this most difficult hour."

She replied, "Thank you, Ash. we'll catch up."

Feeling satisfied, he moved away from her to allow other well-wishers to convey the same to her. Ashman was glad that everything went well and that his conveyance of condolences to her did not raise any suspicions.

At 4 p.m., the burial was completed, and Azmah and her relatives went back home. That night special prayers were to be held for her deceased husband at the mosque. As expected, Ashman attended the Tahlil, or special prayers, at the mosque. Everything went well, and the session ended at 9.30. Again, his presence there didn't raise any eyebrows, even though he tried to look for her at the ladies section of the mosque. He saw Azmah being cool, calm, and composed, though sadness crept in.

The period of mourning for Azmah as a widow was four months and ten days. She was not supposed to go out of the house unnecessarily, except for work. This didn't sit well for both of them. Ashman and Azmah had to bide their time until the mourning period was over. Ashman would text and sometimes call her to keep abreast with developments. The return from haj for both of them involved trying periods, but it was also a blessing in disguise from Allah. As a self-disciplined person, Ashman would patiently wait until the mourning period was over before making any further moves.

Azmah was busy and had to struggle with the problems of managing her two grown-up sons. She had to play the dual roles of mother and father. Her dad, Abdul Aziz, was in his late seventies but took more interest in her family matters. Her father, who lived in Seremban, was a former army officer but considered moving to Kuala Lumpur upon the death of his son-in-law; he wanted to act as a fatherly figure to his daughter and grandsons.

Azmah subtly told him that she had reservations about him moving into her house. This was conveyed through her mother, who was sympathetic to her in light of current events.

As days went by, Azmah was more or less in solitary confinement. Being a homemaker rather than a career woman didn't do her any good, but Ashman was always willing to lend an ears to any problems that she might encounter. That arrangement lessened her burden to a certain extent and kept them in close communication with each other. Occasionally she would visit the graveyard of her late hubby and recite Yaasin for him with her two sons, Amri and Amran, who were always wary of what their mother did. She held her head high to be in control of her own destiny. Her two sons were now studying in college, and the financing of their studies was well arranged by their late father.

One day, Ashman met her at Jaya Shopping Centre in PJ because she was doing some grocery shopping. She was alone without any of her sons, and she looked more radiant than the last couple of weeks. With a feeling of joy, he invited her for a cup of coffee. She was a bit reluctant because her edah was not yet over. After a little persuasion, she agreed and stayed for fifteen minutes, just to catch a breather; no serious matters were discussed. Throughout the meeting, they spoke about normal matters, such as family life after the haj. After the last sip of coffee, she asked to be excused. As she was leaving, he told her, "Take care, Az."

She replied, "Thank you, my dear Ash."

The long-awaited mourning period was soon over for Azmah, and Ashman called her in the morning to say hello. He conveyed to her how relieved he was that the period was over. It was love in the air again for both of them. He told her over the cell phone,

"It's springtime again, dear, and I am looking forward to our renewed relationship."

Initially she was modest about it because the period was over just the previous day, and Malay custom would describe it as a secondary mourning when the deceased's graveyard was still fresh with flowers. After some warming up in their conversation, she was now the person she used to be.

As they went through a longer conversation this time, he told her, "Do you still remember earlier on in our relationship, when I told you that if we could work something out among ourselves, life would be different?"

She replied, "Yes, for sure. It has always been on my mind since then. You also told me that castles could be built in the air." Their conversation was ended abruptly when there was a call from her dad.

On resumption of their conversation ten minutes later, she told him that her dad wanted to drop over at the house over the weekend.

"Anything in particular that your dad wants to discuss with you?" asked Ashman.

"Just a normal visit, but I do not want to discuss any serious matters with him."

"That's okay. I am sure you are able to handle that."

While renewing their chit-chatting sessions, she told him that she was looking forward to meeting him at his convenience, rather than the reverse. With that, they ended their conversation, and he would advise her when and where to meet, after her dad's visit.

The scheduled meet-up between Azmah and her husband in waiting was conveyed to her after her dad left for Seremban, but her mum stayed on for a couple of days. PJ Hilton Hotel was always a nostalgic place for both of them, and the Chinese restaurant seemed to be a properly secluded spot, hidden away from prying eyes. She was delighted and would meet him for a Chinese dinner with four or five courses on a Monday night.

She told her mum that she was going to have dinner with an old friend. She did not disclose to her whom she was meeting, but her mum's motherly instincts suggested that she might be seeing someone. Her mother managed to cajole her. Azmah's two sons were still in college, and the time was now suitable for her to meet Ashman. The meeting went on as schedule, and he waited for her at the basement car park, walked her up to the lobby, and headed straight to the lifts. She was wearing a green modern baju kurung and looked gorgeous in that outfit. Coincidentally, he was wearing a green shirt and matching pants. This was their first meaningful meeting since coming back from the haj.

At the Chinese restaurant, they booked a room, and Ashman didn't know where to start. She started casually with a few stories of home until discussion got underway. He asked her,

"How about Amri and Amran? Would they be comfortable with us seeing each other?"

She replied. "It's too early to say, but Amran can be persuaded. It's best we do not rush this matter."

"I can understand that, but let us play it by the ear and gauge the situation as it goes. You need to play your part in convincing them that life has to go on for you, and them too, after the departure of their father."

Ashman and Azmah fully understood the roles they had to play in the interim to ensure success.

Ash was relating to her what he encountered after the haj. "The haj really changed me a lot, and I became a better person. It taught me to be more patient, but one thing remains: my love for you."

On hearing that, she gave a smile and told him, "You have my assurance that I love you with all my heart. There are no words to describe it."

"Would you be prepared for the hindrances that come along our path?"

"Yes, I'll go for broke."

He then said to her, "We have come a long way to be in this position, and we are not going to lose this position, come what may."

She nodded and told him, "I want you to be my man, whatever it takes. What about Ashley? Is she comfortable with this arrangement?"

He replied, "She is my driving force and would welcome you. I have not told her whom I am seeing at the moment." She looked delightful upon hearing that. After their pledges, the evening was filled with high hopes, aspirations, and emotions.

Throughout the dinner, Ashman maintained his good conduct and never took any advantage of her; they only shook lands. There was no gentle touch on her hand, let alone hugs and kisses. He wanted her to be his angel from paradise, untouched by any man before. He wanted it that way until the marriage solemnisation was over and he heard, "The groom may kiss the bride."

The evening ended on a successful note, and after dinner he ushered her to the lobby and car park to see her off safely. Before she drove off, Ashman said to her,

"Good day, my dear. I love you."

She smiled and answered, "Thank you. I love you too."

Back home in Kota Damansara, Azmah's mum was waiting for her while watching TV. Upon seeing her still in the living room of the house, Azmah said, "Mum, are you not retiring for bed yet?"

She replied, "No, dear. I wasn't that sleepy, so I watched TV while waiting you to get back."

It was now eleven at night, and Azmah sensed her mum could be very inquisitive, but she was prepared for it.

"I am sleepy now, Mum. Maybe tomorrow morning we can talk over breakfast."

Her mum was not too pleased with her coming back late. Off they went to bed, with her mum occupying the room downstairs. Before retiring, Azmah managed to call him to relate what happened. Ashman advised her to be cool and take it naturally, because questions would be asked.

The following morning, Azmah prepared breakfast for her mum, which was toast bread with butter and jam, coffee, and some fruits. At the breakfast table, her mum asked general questions and then went a bit further by asking Azmah of her future plans.

"It's too early to commit to anything, Mum, because my memories with the deceased are still lingering in my mind."

Her mum added that in case she was looking forward to starting life anew, there would be proposals and suitors awaiting.

"Thank you, Mum. You know that since those days and my marriage to the deceased, I would like to have a choice of my own even if Dad had reservations on this matter."

Her mum told her, "Dad was also thinking of that, but we want you to be happy rather than make a wrong move."

"I understand, but this time around, I still would do the same. I hope you and Dad can pray for me as usual, and I seek your blessing."

At the end of the breakfast session, her mum smiled and asked her, "Are you seeing anybody for the moment, or do you have anyone in mind?"

Initially Azmah was lost for an answer, but after some thought, she told her, "I will let you know when the time comes. But you have to tell Dad to not suggest anyone to me, because I would like my own choice."

Her mum nodded and gave assurance that she would talk it over with her dad upon returning to Seremban. With that, she hugged her mum and said,

"Thank you. I love you."

On the day of her mum's departure, she drove her back to Seremban. Dad was not in the house, and after a while Azmah left for Kuala Lumpur.

After the meet-up at PJ Hilton, Ashman continued to be in contact with her and strengthened the relationship. At times he would meet Azmah for grocery shopping at Jaya Supermarket or elsewhere within the vicinity. Whether they were seen by others didn't bother them now. Their contact by phone was almost every night, and by now Ashley was convinced that her dad was seeing someone. One day she told her dad,

"Perhaps it's time now that you let me know who the person is that has captured your heart."

His immediate response was, "Yes, I have one person who has captured my heart, and her name is Azmah, an old friend."

She asked, "What kind of woman is she?"

"She is a widow and a homemaker which are the criteria I am looking for."

"Any children?" she asked.

He answered, "Yes, she has two grown-up sons. Both of them are in college locally. In the near future I will introduce you to her." With that the subject matter was put to rest for a while.

That night he called Azmah and relayed his conversation with Ashley. Azmah said, "What was her reaction to this?"

"Relaxed. She looks comfortable with it, and the three of us may meet soon."

She replied, "I am delighted too, Ash. But with my boys I am not sure where to start."

"It's okay, dear. Don't rush them into it, but by now they should be thinking that you might be seeing somebody."

She was relieved upon hearing his advice. "To start with, let us meet the three of us for lunch or dinner."

Ashman arranged a dinner at Windmill Restaurant in Subang Jaya on a Friday night.

The dinner was at eight o'clock, and as usual Ashman and Ashley arrived early and waited for her at the restaurant. When Azmah arrived, they sat at a table in the far corner. He then introduced Azmah to Ashley, and they got along without much protocol. He was happy with the conversation between them. The food was ordered, and all of them went Western minus the wines. Ashley was happy to get to know her dad's soul mate, and whilst eating they spoke of the holidays outside Malaysia. It was past 10.30 when the dinner ended on a positive note. After settling the bill, Ash offered to escort Azmah back to Kota Damansara by following behind her car to ensure she arrived home safely. Ashley would then know where Azmah resided.

The following day, he called Azmah and told her of the next step. They needed to send a message to her family, especially her two sons, and arrange a meeting similar. He told her,

"I have an idea. it would not be a bad idea to hold another Tahlil session, or special prayer, for their late father and invite me with the rest – say, around forty people. That would be some ice-breaking to them, and let their inquisitiveness of me be the questions they ask you."

She replied, "I have been thinking of that too, and now I feel the time is right for me to do so. The last special prayer were some time ago."

The time was set for next Thursday night. Ashman was invited among her close friends and relatives, and he chipped in some money for the small dinner after the prayers. On the day there were forty people, including Azmah, Amri, and Amran, who helped to arrange for the canopy and chairs so the guests could dine outside their house. Ashman was there among the crowd, and when he arrived, he shook hands with the rest already present. Before the prayers started, some of her relatives were trying to recall some faces they had not met before, and here the inquisitiveness began. Ashman was more relaxed, as if he wasn't a stranger to them. Amri and Amran noticed him, as did a few others. As the prayers ended, the guests were ushered to the dinner table under the canopy, and they had their food. One of the guests asked about Ash, and his reply was that he was an old friend of Azmah's.

Soon after the guest, left, the close relatives who were helping her began to compare notes on many matters, including the stranger in blue Baju Melayu (Malay customary dress). Both Azmah's parents were there, and one of the relatives asked about Ashman and whether he was one of her relatives. Initially she kept her silence, and then she told them,

"I am not sure, because I didn't see him. I saw a few men wearing blue."

Even Amri and Amran asked whether he was a member from the mosque nearby that sometimes were invited. She didn't give a direct answer. "Maybe."

Her dad was holding a watching brief not for his late son-in-law's family but for other matters. Her mum knew that she had a statement to make and gave her time; she would talk with her later. The expressions from Amri and Amran were not initially pleasing.

The following day, Azmah felt that she had to let the cat out of the bag to her mum. She confided to her mum about Ashman, whom she knew some time ago as a normal friend. She claimed she had been in communication with him only after Azman Ali had ascended to the celestial abode, and she saw nothing unusual or wrong about it.

"I have been tending to Azman ever since he was sick, and I took special care of him, especially during his final years. I didn't shirk from my responsibilities, let alone betray him."

She added. "I need a man in my life to be my companion, to drown my sorrows after losing Azman so early."

Her mum advised her, "I am very proud that you are a strong lady and took everything in the stride. It's just a matter of time. Be patient, and I will do my part to convince Dad of your wishes. But in the interim, you need to take care of Amri and Amran, and then they will concur with you."

After the heart to heart talk between mum and daughter, she hugged her mum and told her,

"You are one in a million."

Azmah's wishes were conveyed by her mum to her dad in Seremban. The initial reaction was that that he didn't take kindly to such a move, though a lot of persuasion came from her mum. As days went by, Azmah called upon her dad and indicated her interests to remarry a person of her choice. She could understand her dad's reluctance since there were already suitors who were waiting for an answer from her. As a widow, she turned down such proposals, but she did it in a nice manner; still, one or two of them got offended by her rejection. She told them through her dad that she already had a person whom she intended to marry, but this didn't go down well with those in question. At this juncture, her dad would not sanction anyone asking for her hand.

The whole scenario was conveyed to Ashman by Azmah, and she was bewildered by it and sought some solace and guidance from him. Ashman was shocked and hadn't expected the reaction from her dad. He then advised her with some consoling words that provided her with relief over the matter. He advised her to perform special prayers at night, asking Allah for a clear path to proceed in matrimonial arrangements. At times she was in tears during the phone conversation, but he managed to calm her down and advised her to be strong in the face of such adversity.

"We will ride the storm together," he told her. Upon hearing that, she slowly got back to her feet and thanked him for the advice. He added,

"Nothing is more satisfying than to make you happy."

Her reply was, "Oh, I love you, Ash."

The following day, he called her up and told her that he wanted to meet her to discuss the matter. He told her to meet for afternoon tea at Jaya Supermarket. She arrived early this time, eager to meet up with him, and she took a table and sat in the far corner, away from the prying eyes of many. In about ten minutes, Ashman arrived, and her expression was filled with happiness upon seeing him. They sat and order some snacks to go with their coffee.

This time he told her that they had to proceed, whatever it took. "Azmah, my love, would you arrange a meeting with your dad, either in Seremban or at your house?" he asked her.

"Sure," was her reply.

He added, "I will do whatever that is possible for the time being, and you will stand by me."

She nodded and said, "Amran has been supportive lately, but Amri will have to be persuaded."

Evening approached, and they ended the meeting with the hope that Azmah would be successful in arranging the meeting.

Upon reaching home and having a light dinner, Azmah called her dad and started the conversation casually. She relayed the message from Ashman. To her surprise, it drew a blank from her dad. Undeterred by that, she called her mum the following morning and sought her assistance. Her mum lent an ear and would again try to convince her dad, who was adamant against all this. She gave Azmah assurance that she would assist her, but it could take some time.

After a week, there was still no positive answer from him, and finally the following day came an answer from him: he was not prepared to meet Ashman or discuss anything about it. This was relayed to Ashman, who remained calm and composed.

Chapter 15

Crossing the Rubicon

The following afternoon was a Saturday, and Azmah's father and mother decided to drop in under the guise of paying a surprise visit to her, hoping to bump into Ashman. To her surprise, she told her parents,

"Mum and Dad, why didn't you inform me earlier that you were coming to town, so that I could fix a meal for us?"

Her dad, "We didn't want to trouble you so much."

Still amazed and surprised, she remained quiet and asked what their programme was. She went into the kitchen to prepare some refreshments. As they were sitting in the living room, both Amri and Amran appeared from their rooms and greeted their grannies. They sat in the living room until Zohor prayers, and the visitors checked in the guest room.

At dinner time, Azmah told the boys to order some pizza. The two boys were going out with their own programmes. Once the pizza arrived, the three adults sat at the dinner table. Pizza was her dad's favourite Western food. Her mum helped her in the kitchen. Once the pizza was served, they had a hearty meal, and Dad began the conversation after the meal.

"Az, I find it weird that this old friend of yours was in your heart so shortly after Azman passed away."

She answered, "Nothing unusual about that, Dad, because during the funeral, he paid a visit. After that, it blossomed into a friendship."

"Hmm, looks like he has a buyout clause in your marriage contract so that he has the first option to marry you once you are available," her dad said.

Mum interjected, "You are too far ahead and speculating on the future. This is a simple matter, so keep it simple."

Azmah looked cheerful and remained quiet for a while as her mother supported her on this. Her father said,

"Both of you seem to be united in this, but I still have my reservations."

There was some silence for a while, and then Mum told her,

"Let's clear the dishes, and after watching TV, you can go to your room and retire. Maybe we'll leave for Seremban tomorrow morning."

It was almost eleven at night, and Azmah excused herself and went into her room. She texted Ashman that her parents were here and would call him the next day once they left for Seremban.

The next morning, she prepared breakfast with her mum, and the latter gave assurances that she would assist in this matter.

"Your father has been a difficult person lately, and I find him a little bit changed."

After breakfast, Mum and Dad left for Seremban, but there was little to suggest at this point that Dad would give the go-ahead easily.

After they left, she called Ashman and briefly relayed her discussions with her parents. This didn't come as a surprise to him; he'd expected that kind of response. Azmah told him that she wanted to meet up with him in the late afternoon. Their rendezvous had to be changed this time, and he suggested the Hornbill Restaurant, in the vicinity of Lake Gardens, which was a quiet little nook to discuss matters.

As usual, he arrived early and waited for her at the car park. Soon after she arrived, he ushered her to the quaint restaurant with many kind of birds surrounding the patio area, which was ideal for relaxing. There, they sat and discussed all sorts of matters, including serious ones that affected their relationship. She told him of her difficulties lately, and he listened with empathy.

At one juncture he asked her, "What if I were to send some feelers to inquire of your availability?"

She answered, "You can try, but it might be futile because he doesn't agree to meet you."

"Let me do some soul-searching prayers tonight, and I'll let you know of the outcome."

She smiled and agreed. It was almost seven o'clock, and the couple ended their meeting. He walked beside her to the car park, and they held their heads high. She thanked him for spending the afternoon with her. He said,

"I should thank you for keeping me company. I will call you tonight because we do not want to miss each other."

She smiled and said, "Okay, that's fine."

When she returned home, Amri was curious as to where she'd been, but she quashed the matter with a very simple answer. Amri wasn't satisfied with her answer, however she managed to calm him down after some strong advice, and the matter was resolved without much issue.

After nightfall, she waited for Ash to call. He eventually called around ten and told her that he wanted to go through with seeding feelers to her parents. He thought it would be a courteous way of approaching the subject matter according to Islam and Malay culture. She agreed and transmitted all the details to him in order to proceed.

The following day, Ashman called up his relatives to get in touch with her parents in Seremban. Though it wasn't plain sailing as expected, he waited with bated breath for a response, which wasn't forthcoming within the normal time. A second envoy was despatched, but this time the answer came back as a negative. On hearing that, Ashman shook his head and told himself,

"What kind of a person am I dealing with?"

His special envoys consoled him on this and offered their advice, suggesting he create a plan B, but he was unmoved by that for a time being.

After so much deliberation and soul searching, Ashman would have to decide on which direction to proceed. After performing special prayers at night, he was now determined to proceed in the direction he wanted: propose to Azmah and tell her that he wanted to take her as his beloved wife, come what may. He was aware that her younger son, Amri, had eventually been in agreement on this, but the approval from her father wasn't easily obtained. Azmah was also very disturbed by the latest developments, and he prayed hard to Allah. Realising that there were obstacles along the way, Ash decided to consult his Syariah lawyer, Mohamed Chan, and set a date with him.

He dropped into Chan's office after work, and again Chan's greeting was, "What brings you here this time?"

"The less I meet you, the better it is for me, unless we have a cup of coffee together."

After laughing at each other, business started as usual for Chan. Then Ashman related to him what had happened. He told him that Azmah's father objected to their proposed marriage for reasons known only to her father, and he would not sanction the marriage as her wali. He told Chan that this was not the case of her earlier marriage, because it was her choice of man. Chan said,

"I am puzzled how this could have happened. Either her father has a strong dislike for you, or he has somebody else in mind."

Ashman answered, "The latter is probably the case, knowing that Azmah is a woman of beauty and grace."

Chan nodded and advised him that this was a case of wali enggan, or guardian's refusal. After some discussions, Chan advised him on some points.

1. Fill up the application for marriage by both parties, and Azmah could leave blank the portion on guardian's approval.
2. Fill up the guardian's refusal form, which was obtained from the Religious Department.
3. Submit both forms to the officer.

Chan added that if Ash chose this procedure, then the department would call her guardian to the court and listen to his explanation by way of summons. If the guardian didn't turn up in court, a second summons would be issued, and subsequently a third. After the third summons, failure to turn up would result in the court deciding based on the merits of the case. If all conditions were met, the court would appoint a wali hakim, or royal guardian, to solemnise the marriage. This would be a painstaking process, but it would be a legal remedy for the dilemma.

Alternatively, Chan advised him that they could solemnise the marriage in Perlis using the royal guardian without going through the above. The states of Malaysia were independent on their own, and Perlis had waived the guardian's consent and elected for the royal guardian. There was also another way that would entail solemnisation the marriage in Southern Thailand, but the certificate would be issued by Thai authorities. One needed to reregister in Malaysia after that and pay a small fine, and the case would be heard in chambers. Those were options available for him.

Ashman shook his head in dismay and told himself, "Why would a simple procedure undergo a complicated web of procedures – something of a good cause and encouraged by Islam?"

After much deliberation with Chan, he left the lawyer's office and headed home. There he was greeted by Ashley, who asked him to go out for dinner. He managed to hide his frustrations and joined her for dinner, this time at Kelantan Delights Restaurant in Subang Jaya, famed for its Kelantan cuisine. At the restaurant over dinner, he confided the whole matter to Ashley, who by now was a mature young lady able to comprehend and digest most of the intricacies of married life. She lent her ears to him and pledged to be with him in these difficult situations. She told him, "I am with you, Dad." Upon hearing that, Ashman was relieved.

After dinner, they went straight home. After showers and prayers, he called Azmah. She was also shocked to hear what he'd relayed to her. By now she was fully aware of the procedures. They discussed it over the phone, and Ashman wanted to meet up with her the following late afternoon. They would meet again at the Hornbill Restaurant. This time Ashman suggested that she bring along her jogging suit to have a brisk walk around the nearby Lake Gardens of Kuala Lumpur.

She turned up on time and arrived early. In a couple of minutes, Ashman came. For the first time, they were seen jogging together in the vicinity of the lake. After a while, they stop at one of the benches along the jogging track to catch a breather and enjoy the beautiful scenery in the early evening. After twenty minutes, they continued in the form of brisk walk towards the Hornbill Restaurant.

At the restaurant, they changed out of their jogging attire and discussed things at length over tea in the excellent ambience of the bird park, where the hornbills roamed free. Both of them concurred that going for option one by calling her father to court would be unthinkable in light of present circumstances. In all fairness, it wasn't the best option; she could be disowned by her father, which was the last thing they wanted. They thought the second option was probably worth considering.

Before they left the restaurant, he asked her, "Apart from your dad, who else is not comfortable with our marriage plan?"

She answered, "Only my father, and his attitude was more worrying. Amri would eventually be supportive despite being very possessive."

"Good, then it's only one person. We shall think on which option will be less damaging to him."

No decision was made at the Hornbill Restaurant, and they ended the tea meeting in the late evening. As usual, he walked with her but without holding hands. They looked more like a romantic couple, and facial expressions suggested that love was in the air. Both were going back home for further soul searching over the matter.

At night they performed the special soul-searching prayers and were in contact over the phone. Though nothing came through, they kept hope and walked with their heads held high. She waited for him on the proposed course of action as the days went by.

In the interim, Ashman consulted his close relatives and friends on the matter, and he obtained some encouragement from them. One day he called Mohamed Chan and updated him on his current status. The following night, he called Azmah and updated her on the scenario.

She answered,

"Thank you, Ash. I love you so much."

They were on the line for ten minutes, and before ending the conversation, she said,

"I leave everything to you for our future. Goodnight, dear, and lots of love."

Azmah confided this to her best friend, Zaini Harun, and she received lots of advice and encouragement. Zaini had been another pillar of strength for her. At times she would drop by Azmah's house, and the pair seemed to be jovial together, forgetting the problems surrounding them. At every opportunity, Zaini counselled Amri and Amran, and the results were encouraging. However, there seemed to be an improvement from both of them towards their mum's proposed marriage. At one juncture, she told Amri,

"Your mum need a person to take care of her as a partner and companion. That would benefit all parties."

Amri could only remain silent, but she managed to convince Amran, and she had been instrumental for the change in stance. She added,

"Your matrimonial life will come someday, and you will better understand the situation."

Those words were music to Azmah's ears, and Amri took it with an open heart.

Time seemed to be a standstill for the loving couple, who were eager to tie the matrimonial knot. Ashman pondered on the matter more, and at last he said to himself,

"If the mountain does not come to Muhammad, then Muhammad will go to the mountain."

Based on that premise, he was ready to decide the next course of action. Undeterred by anything, he was now fully determined to marry Azmah in the state of Perlis using a royal guardian procedure. One afternoon, he called her to meet at the new rendezvous at the Hornbill Restaurant to break the news of his audacious decision. Azmah was glad that he wanted to take that bold step and solemnise the marriage in Perlis.

At the meeting, he told her,

"With all the love to you, I am taking a bold step towards making our dreams come through, God willing."

She replied, "I am here for you."

He needed those comforting words from her as a boost that inspired him further.

"I would like to emulate Julius Caesar centuries ago, when he took a valiant step to cross the Rubicon. It is a point of no return with calculated risks."

She nodded as a sign of agreement and gave him a huge smile.

Ashman soon remembered that when he told his close friends about crossing the Rubicon, a few advised him to be careful because,

"The graveyards are full of heroes".

Undeterred by the word of caution, he detailed to Azmah the modus operandi. With that, they ended the meeting because it was almost nightfall. He walked beside her to their cars, ending a successful afternoon meeting. They decided to perform the Magrib prayers at the nearby National Mosque. After prayers, Ashman and Azmah headed back home, feeling relieved and more relaxed. He followed her car back to her house in Kota Damansara and saw her off before returning to his house in Section 11, Petaling Jaya.

Chapter 16

The Bride in Waiting

The plan to solemnise their marriage in Perlis was to be a secret, confidential arrangement known only between them, Mohamed Chan, and Zaini Harun. Even Ashley didn't know in the initial stages. Ashman met Chan to discuss the procedures and other paperwork related to the matter. Discussions were held in Chan's office, and for the first time he brought Azmah along to have a feel of the matter. It was a Saturday afternoon, and the plan was hatched for the couple to follow. Chan would assist in the paperwork and would travel along with him to Perlis. Azmah would fly to Perlis via Alor Star under the pretext of visiting her close friend Zaini, who was a resident of the state.

Preparations were underway with painstaking details being worked towards the ultimate goal of marrying in the state of Perlis. Ashman was known to be a detailed person who would perform due diligence for the matters involved. In short, there were no stones left unturned. He and Azmah met at Chan's office to further discuss the matter, including logistics, while Ashman took care of all the finances. Back home, Azmah would choose a suitable dress for the occasion. The solemnisation would take place at the State Religious

Department in Kangar, Perlis. The colour theme would be yellow and white, with no frills this time around.

She looked radiant when trying out the outfit at her house, and her luggage was packed and sent through Ashman as a decoy. The date had yet to be fixed by the state authorities, but Mohamed Chan pressed for the earliest possible date. She kept in communication with her buddy Zaini Harun, and initial arrangements were made that she would stay at Zaini's house to avoid being detected by others. Chan would book the hotel room for two in case Azmah wanted to take up the room for a last-minute change; if that was the case, he would share the room with Ashman. They planned to do a little shopping at the border town of Padang Besar, which was a must for tourists.

Ashman then thought about whether they would want to have a small reception back home. He told her, "Yes, we could do a small one at my house, and following that, one at your house once everything is settled."

She smiled and was delighted to hear that.

"I will invite my close relatives and friends only."

"That's good. We shall announce that we are now legally wedded." was his reply.

But inside, Ashman felt it was too soon to speak out on that because there were obstacles to be cleared. Still, he wanted to provide her with a morale boost.

After receiving news on the clearance of the paperwork from Kangar, Perlis, Chan informed him, and they discussed the details and plans for the solemnisation of the marriage. As discussed between them and Azmah, also in attendance, they decided that the following week was suitable, and it would be carried out on a Sunday, which was working day in

Perlis. The party would leave KL the day before via a flight from Subang Airport, using Firefly Airways to Alor Star. The plan was hatched that Zaini Harun would pay a visit to her a few days earlier, and Azmah would reciprocate the visit to Kangar. During Zaini's stay as a host to Azmah, the latter told Amri and Amran that she would pay a return visit to Zaini in Kangar. She had to show excitement to her children because this was her first visit to Perlis, and she might do a little shopping at Padang Besar. Her sons took it plainly and never suspected anything.

Over at Ashman's house, he applied for leave on the following Monday because the return flight was to be on a Monday morning. There was little packing to do for his suitcase, which was always ready because he was a man on the go. He cleared his office work early in order to have a clear mind on the marriage, and only his elder brother knew about it. Ashley was not to be told yet because he didn't want it to affect her studies. In between, he performed special prayers at night in his house after coming back from the mosque, seeking divine help from Allah. He then told Ashley that he would be going to Alor Star for a short trip and would be back by Monday. In his mind, he didn't want her mum to know, should there be a slip of the tongue. Up to then, Ashman did all the due diligence to ensure a smooth passage. He even had a contingency plan in case of a last-minute postponement, which was common in the State Religious Department.

The preceding Saturday was the trip from Subang Airport to Alor Star, and Azmah and Zaini were to leave by a morning flight. The latter's relatives were to pick them up at Alor Star for Kangar. They were to board Malindo Air and had an open return tickets. Both of them took a cab while Amri and Amran were at college. As planned, Ashman and Mohamed Chan would take the afternoon flight by Firefly Airways. As it turned out, it was a smooth journey for the ladies, but for the men there was a slight delay of two hours due to bad weather. Ashman told himself after checking in at Subang, "Is this an indication of things to come?" He had never been superstitious before, but this gut feeling was in him throughout the waiting time at the departure hall. Chan didn't notice anything.

In the interim, he called Azmah and said, "How are you getting on there? I hope you are comfortable being the guest of Zaini."

"What a coincidence – I was about to call you. Yes, I am comfortable here, and Zaini treats me well. Her hospitality is worth mentioning."

He then told her of the flight delay.

"Don't worry, dear. It's just a normal delay due to bad weather. Chan is keeping me company. Okay, the boarding announcement is made. I will call you again once we arrived in Alor Star."

Once the gates were opened, the two men walked along the corridor outside the terminal building to the aircraft parked nearby. Ashman could see the dark clouds hovering around the sky, and he remained silent but calm. He chanted his prayers for a successful trip to Perlis.

Once on board, they took seats at the front of the aircraft. It was almost 3.15 p.m., and the journey to Alor Star would take approximately an hour. From there, it was another hour to reach Kangar, the capital of Perlis. Kangar did not a have an airport of its own, and that reminded Ash that Leeds shared the same airport as Bradford, which was known as Leeds/Bradford Airport, unlike Liverpool's John Lennon International Airport.

At 4.40 local time, they arrived at Alor Star Airport at Kepala Batas. As they disembarked from the aircraft, the weather was sunny skies with a temperature of 34 degree Celsius. Ashman held his head high just like the lyrics in the song "You'll Never Walk Alone". With high hopes from the husband-elect of the bride, he moved quickly as his old buddy, Hakimi Musa was ready to take him to Kangar. They were so eager to reach Kangar before sunset that they didn't stop for any refreshments.

It was almost 5.45 hours when the entourage reached Kangar, and they had a late afternoon tea at Zaini's residence, where English scones and earl grey tea were served. These were Ashman's favourites during his Liverpool days, which was a pleasant surprise to him. It was courtesy of an idea by his would be life partner. In a more relaxed atmosphere, they discussed the plan for tomorrow. Upon completing the discussion, Ashman chanted a few prayers for a successful solemnisation. They left Zaini's residence at 6.45, and Ashman and Chan checked in at Kangar's Seri Malaysia Hotel, a local version of Traveller's Lodge. Hakimi took them to the hotel. Hakimi was a local boy and once worked with the United Engineering Berhad; he was now doing his own business in Bukit Ketri, not far from Kangar. Hakimi and Ashman's bond remained strong, which was why Hakimi was the man entrusted to carry out this project.

When they checked in at Seri Malaysia, it was almost 7 p.m. Ashman shared the room with Chan, and Hakimi took another room beside them. It was almost time for the Magrib prayers, and Hakimi suggested that they have a quiet dinner at the hotel without the ladies being called. It was agreed, and Hakimi's wife was at Zaini's residence too. They also discussed that it would be safe and unsuspecting that the bride in waiting continued to stay at Zaini's residence instead of taking up another room with Zaini at the hotel. Ashman kept communicating with Azmah. Meanwhile Azmah, called Amri and Amran, telling them that she'd arrived safely at Zaini's residence, and she advised them not to worry. So far all of Ashman's plan had worked without a hitch. Any idea of celebration, no matter how small, had to be done after the solemnisation tomorrow.

The three gentleman had dinner at Seri Malaysia and relaxed afterwards. As usual, Ashman managed to call Ashley and told her that he'd just had dinner with his business colleagues at the hotel and would return in two days. Over coffee they made small talk, and Hakimi caught up with Ashman over their early careers at the United Engineering Berhad. Before they retired for the night, Ashman again called up Azmah and briefed her on what had to be done tomorrow morning. They'd commence at 9.30 at the Religious Department, and they would meet at 9.00. She would come in one car with Zaini and Hakimi's wife, Zalifah, and Hikimi would take Ashman and Chan in his car.

"Good night dear, my bride in waiting," were his last words to her for the day. Her reply was,

"Goodnight Ash and lots of love"

They both retired and called it a day. It was a very romantic atmosphere to end the day, and the couple looked forward to the following day with high hopes.

Chapter 17

The Moment of Truth

That Sunday morning at 5.30 a.m., most of them were awake to perform the Suboh prayers. The moment of truth then set in, and Azmah surprisingly received a call from her father that he was at the front gate of Zaini's residence, asking her to come back to KL with him immediately.

"You come out of the house now, or else my two commando friends will storm in and force you out of the house."

Her father was as mean as ever. Azmah was speechless and did not want to create a scene. She asked Zaini, who was in the bathroom, for advice. After a couple of minutes, Azmah replied to her father.

"Do not embarrass me because I am a guest of Zaini's. I am here, and it is not what you think."

Abdul Aziz retorted, "I don't care. You are coming back with me."

She then agreed to surrender to her father. Zaini opened the front door as the trio barged in like uncivilised hooligans, and in a few seconds they managed to subdue Azmah with a chemical that rendered her unconscious. She was carried to a waiting car to take her back to KL. It happened so quickly that Zaini and Zalifah were dumbfounded, speechless, and frightened. It was executed with military precision thanks to Azmah's father, who was formerly military intelligence in the army.

After regaining composure, Zalifah called Hakimi and relayed to him what had taken place. Hakimi was speechless for a while, trying to figure out on how to break this news to Ashman, who was in the next room.

Bad news had to be told, and so Hakimi knocked on his door. Chan opened the door because Ashman was in the shower. Chan looked puzzled and asked him what was wrong, but Hakimi said he would rather wait until Ashman came out.

When Ashman walked out of the shower room, he was perplexed as to why Hakimi and Chan were quiet. "What is the problem, Hakimi?" he asked.

"We have to postpone this solemnisation or cancel it, because Azmah was abducted by her father twenty minutes ago and driven back to KL. He was assisted by commando friends."

"What!" exclaimed Ashman as he chanted a prayer to calm himself. He then turn around to Chan and said,

"What is your advice on this matter? Shall we report it to the police?"

Chan managed to cool Ashman further and said,

"Let us do our Suboh prayer together and discuss this matter after that." They agreed and performed Suboh prayers together.

Afterwards, Chan took centre stage and began explaining.

"This is a conflict of legal matters. Even if you make a police report on the abduction and subsequently false imprisonment, matters of matrimonial arrangements would be dealt under the Syariah law that the wali, or guardian, has to give permission. This is where calling the guardian to Syariah court to explain the objections will have to take due course."

This was the very process that Ashman had wanted to avoid in the first place, and it'd turned out to work against him.

"What do I do now?" asked Ashman.

Chan replied,

"Relax, my friend. We have other options to work. This is where your plan B has to be considered."

In the interim, Hakimi called his wife, who was still at Zaini's residence, and told her to relax. The trio would be coming over for breakfast to discuss the matter. Fifteen minutes later, they arrived at Zaini's residence. The women were still preparing breakfast, but Zalifah came out to make the men feel comfortable and told them what had happened more than an hour ago.

"It was shocking and terrifying, which came as a rude awakening to us in the wee hours of the morning."

Zaini expressed her dismay and added,

"Azmah was in tears and tatters before they subdued her with some chemical substance and carried her into a white Mitsubishi Pajero."

Ashman had a forlorn expression on his face but kept his cool.

They further discussed the matter as breakfast was prepared. As the others tried to console Ashman, he said,

"This is very unprecedented drama in matrimonial history, reminiscent of the same tragedy that had befallen

Mansor Adabi and Natrah in 1950 in Singapore, which was followed by religious riots. The only difference is they didn't give Azmah holy water to drink."

After a while, Ashman thanked Zaini for her kind hospitality and apologised to her for these incidents that took place in her residence.

She replied, "Oh, don't thank me. I felt sorry for the how Azmah was treated."

Ashman then told Hakimi to head for the Perlis Religious Department to postpone the solemnisation event. He and Chan would return to KL on the earliest flight.

Half an hour later, Hakimi returned after settling the matters with the Religious Department, but not without getting a ticking from those officers. As a local man, it was the lightest ticking. Soon after he took the duo to the hotel, and they checked out of the hotel, looking melancholy and dejected at the failed mission. Ashman would have to do some post-mortem and soul searching, and he'd later plan a course of action to pursue. With that, they bid farewell to Zaini and Zalifah as Hakimi drove the duo to Alor Star to catch the return flight to KL. Zalifah stayed back with Zaini to provide company to the host and comfort her in any way she could.

Along the way, he thought about how on earth would Azmah's father knew about their plan, and how he could hijack their plans in the eleventh hour. Either the information was leaked, or her father heard that she was going to Kangar for a visit to Zaini's residence and had a sixth sense. All these were mind-boggling to him and were things he did not foresee during his risk management analysis earlier. As a planning engineer by profession, no stones should have been left unturned. Chan was quiet during the journey, waiting to answer any questions that Ash might have.

Ashman and Chan remained quiet at the departure hall. Chan bought some drinks and snacks to quench their thirst, and Ashman had a sip of a drink. At the departure hall, he looked towards the tarmac of the airport, and he could see some dark clouds being formed. It crossed his mind that before the journey to Alor Star, he remembered dark clouds hovering in the sky at Subang. He said to himself,

"Are these dark clouds a prelude to a drama or tragedy to come?"

As he waited for the flight to depart which was delayed by another thirty minutes, Ashman felt that was the longest wait he's ever had at the airport. Nothing else sprang from his mind other than the devilish act from Azmah's father, who would be an octogenarian by the middle of the year. He worried about what would happen to his bride in waiting after being abducted. He would want to conduct his own post-mortem on that fateful incident at Zaini's residence; he vowed that those responsible would be dealt with by the law. Meanwhile, he called on Ashley to inform her that he would be returning to KL earlier than expected. Then he boarded the flight back to Subang Airport in a pensive mood.

Azmah's journey back to KL by road was a smooth one. As she woke up from her long slumber due to the tranquiliser, the Pajero was driven out from Kangar and made a stop en route at the Sungai Perak rest area at eight in the morning. She woke up to find herself in the rear seat with her vicious father; the two former commandoes were in the front seats. Out of anger, she remained silent and did not want to talk to anyone in the vehicle, not even her dad, whom she regarded him as a wolf in a sheep's clothing. She soon realised that her cell phone was missing, but her guess was right: that her dad had kept her cell phone and turned it off. She soon realised that her dad's army instincts had not faded despite of his age.

As the party was about to resume the journey to KL, she requested to go to the ladies' room. She told them cynically,

"I want to go to the ladies' to answer the call of nature, or I'll do my business here."

Her dad had to be her chaperone and was assisted by one commando, Zainuddin Abdul Rahim.

After fifteen minutes, she didn't come out of the room, and her dad sought help from other woman to look for her inside. The woman entrusted to check for her told him that she was recovering after vomiting blood and needed some time to be on her own. On hearing that, Abdul Aziz wanted to go inside to pull her out, but he was restrained by a women. The three of them waited impatiently outside the bathroom with some curious onlookers wondering at the scene. After twenty minutes, Azmah walked out of the ladies very slowly with another woman holding her hand. The trio was not amused by that, and neither did they have any sympathy for her. She walked to the Pajero assisted by the same woman.

Inside the Pajero, Azmah felt that she was like a wanted terrorist being escorted by two former commandoes; her father was acting like one too. She asked her father for her cell phone to call Amri and Amran, but he denied her request and said,

"Everything is being taken care of. I will change your cell phone number once we reach KL."

Not wanting to argue over it, she remained silent but refused any food and drinks offered to her. She didn't answer any other questions from her father, who looked satisfied for his mission accomplished.

To her surprise, she wasn't taken back to Kota Damansara, and she soon realised that they were taking her back to her father's house in Seremban. "What a startling development!" she told herself.

"Oh, God, what have I done to deserve this?"

Her mother, Rahimah Abdul Rahman, was eagerly waiting in Seremban. When the news reached her, she was ready to console and comfort her only daughter. She was still unable to comprehend the actions taken by her husband, who was known to be highly temperamental. This time she failed to reason with him, and she could only pray for the best. Upon reaching Seremban, Azmah was exhausted and almost fainted as she was helped by her mother to enter the house. There were tears in her mother's eyes as she looked to her husband with sheer astonishment.

Azmah's woes did not end in her parents' home in Seremban but it was just a beginning to another chapter in her life. After the long journey and vomiting, she dashed into the guest room and locked herself in and slept the whole day. Only her mother was attending to her soon after.

Chapter 18

Enter the Trojan Horse

Back home in PJ, Ashman called Amran over the cell phone and asked the whereabouts of his mum. Amran was puzzled about what had actually happened. After being told by Ashman, Amran now understood the whole story and promised to call him once he got some info. The best person to call was his grandmother in Seremban, whom he trusted.

"No wonder there was no answer when I called my mum yesterday. I thought she'd switched off her cell phone for reasons best known to her," he said.

In less than an hour, he learned about what had happened through his grandmother, and he was sad about the drastic and tragic action taken by his grandfather.

Amran relayed the message to Ashman, who received the news with a tinge of sadness, but Ash was a little relieved to know where Azmah was.

"Thanks, Amran. I know that I can count on you," he told Amran.

Amran also discreetly told him of the address in Seremban and the house's phone number. Ashman had a busy day trying to calm himself over the tragedy. He was still on leave and decided to add another day. Not since Ashfah had betrayed him many years ago had he had a tragic experience in his life. These two tragedies would always be in his mind to the end, and they left a black hole in his chequered life.

The following day, he was back in office trying to wash away the sorrow. At noon, he didn't go for lunch and instead stayed in his room, plotting the next move. It was back to the drawing board for him, and a few ideas came out. He decided to try out some of them.

Hakimi, who was based in Perlis, came to town for a short visit, and Ash invited him for dinner to discuss the next move. Ashman told him of the plan, and Hakimi was all for it. They decided to pay a visit to Seremban to recce the situation in an attempt to find out what had happened to his bride in waiting. On Friday, Ashman took leave and travelled in his friend's motorcar with Hakimi to Seremban. They arrived at noon to coincide with the Friday prayers. With the address given by Amran, they drove to Taman Bukit Kaya, which was an old residential area. They soon arrived at the exact address which was facing a green field – an ideal place for some espionage work. The house number was seventeen, and it was a small cottage house with matured trees. Azmah's father, which Ashman referred him as Abdul Aziz the Great for his prowess in the Perlis operation, hailed from Batu Pahat and had since moved to Seremban to reside at Azmah's mother's hometown.

Hakimi stayed inside the car as Ashman wandered in the open field. This was a perfect spot to put on surveillance of the house, and it was a chance to have a glimpse of Azmah. Before long, Abdul Aziz came out of the house and drove his car to attend the weekly Friday prayers. Azmah was not to be seen as yet, and Ashman waited patiently for her to come out. After five minutes, he decided to call the house phone, but her mother picked up the phone because Azmah was not allowed to answer.

"Good afternoon, aunty. This is Ashman. May I speak to Azmah, please?"

There was a silent moment. Her mum was surprised but passed the line to her after replying to Ashman,

"Hello, Ash. okay, I'll pass the line to her."

"Azmah here," was the faint reply.

Ashman said, "Relax, dear. I am here just outside your house under the tree in the green field. Have a look outside, and you will be able to see Hakimi inside the car, with me under a tree."

Azmah was ecstatic with joy on hearing that, and she peeked outside the house and saw who was there. She was brimming with a tinge of happiness and continued the conversation. "Please do not come close to the house, because dad just bought an Alsatian to guard the house. I am all right and have recovered slightly since the debacle in Perlis."

He replied, "Wow! I never thought his army instincts would come this far, or that he'd really put you under house arrest."

Azmah told him of what had happened on the fateful day, and she was recovering slowly due to the tragic situation.

He then asked her,

"Can you come out of the house right now?"

"No, I'm quite afraid because my father has installed a CCTV and monitors my movements inside and outside the house."

Ashman was speechless on hearing that but continued the conversation with her. Finally he asked her to look out of the house just to get a glimpse of each other. She obliged, and they were reunited with glimpses of each other for seven minutes before she went in. He assured her that he would do his best to resolve the matter and tie the matrimonial knot, God willing.

In the interim, Ashman told her to find ways for her to communicate with him, either directly or through Amran, when the time was right. He would also communicate his plans and next move discreetly.

"Is your mum on our side?" he asked her, and her reply was in the affirmative. "Good. Pray to Allah so that our wishes would come true." Those were his last words of the conversation.

After the lengthy conversation with Azmah, he joined Hakimi inside the car he'd borrowed from an office colleague to avoid detection. Once inside the car, he relayed to Hakimi what had transpired, and that surprised Hakimi even more. Hakimi jokingly told him,

"You need an army to break into that house, Ash."

His reply was, "Hmm. I don't need an army, but I need a Trojan horse to do the job for me."

They decided to leave the place and head for town to have a quick lunch before her father came back from Friday prayers. True to expectations, her father returned shortly after prayers but did not suspect anything, and Azmah remained in a natural state.

Back in PJ, Ashman told Hakimi that he wanted to send a high-powered delegation to Abdul Aziz's house seeking forgiveness if any of his actions offended him, and also asking for Azmah's hand for marriage.

"Who do have in mind to send?" asked Hakimi, and there was no immediate answer from Ashman.

After a while Ash told him,

"I have this ambassador friend from one of the Gulf States who was with me at John Moores University, Liverpool. He's always willing to give a helping hand should I approach him."

Hakimi was not amused by that and told him,

"If I may suggest something? In true Malaysian tradition, you should get someone close to her family, like her uncle or her father's friends."

"Frankly speaking, I would like to try something different. Besides, Azmah told me none of her relatives would be willing to undertake the job knowing her father's behaviour.

After some soul searching and due diligence, Ashman planned to proceed with sending a high-powered delegation headed by his ambassador friend. The next day, he called upon his Liverpool colleague at John Moores University and set up a meeting with him at the ambassador's residence in Ampang.

"What brings you here?" asked the ambassador after they had a cup of coffee.

Ashman related old memories during their varsity days, and they smiled and laughed at the good old days they'd had together at the Merseyside, although the ambassador was an ardent Everton fan and still supported the club.

The ambassador then said, "I believe this is not the purpose of our meeting today?"

"I have something else to bring up, and I think you are in a position to help me," replied Ashman.

"Okay, shoot," said the ambassador.

On hearing that, Ashman related to him what had happened. The ambassador told him,

" Ashman, I feel sorry to hear that, but how would you want me to help you on this matter?"

Ashman told him of his plans, and the ambassador told him,

"Not to worry, my friend. I shall use my best endeavours to help you as per your plan. Even so, pray to Allah for success."

All the details were given to the ambassador, and Ashman was to advise him on when to commence.

The following week the high-powered delegation would meet Azmah's father in Seremban. After a few days, Abdul Aziz received the request for an audience by His Excellency, the Ambassador Extraordinary and Plenipotentiary of one of the Gulf States. There was no way he could refuse, and he reluctantly accepted the request after seeking a few clarifications on the purpose of the visit. The meeting was set up for a Friday afternoon at 3.30, just after Friday prayers. The ambassador was accompanied by his Lady in a Mercedes S Class, and he was escorted by police outriders. Abdul Aziz was eager to meet the delegation because he could put the matter to rest once and for all. He told Azmah that Ashman would be sending a high-powered delegation to meet with him over the matter. Azmah received it with mixed feelings but hoped for a good outcome.

On the agreed day and time, the entourage arrived in true style and protocol to Abdul Aziz's residence in Taman Bukit Kaya. They were received with open arms by the hosts, which comprised Azmah's father and mother; also in attendance was her close aunty. As the dignitaries arrived, His Excellency greeted the hosts with "Assalamualaikum" in the true Muslim way. They reply was, "Waalaikumusssalam." As the distinguished guests were ushered to their seats in the living room, the usual formalities and etiquettes were observed. The ambassador, who was dressed in the traditional Arab jubah, or robe, presented the host with a gift in a form of Arab luxury robes that could be used for prayers for both the host and his wife. In return, the host presented a pewter platter as a souvenir to the distinguished guests.

After the brief exchange of gifts, the ambassador sought the host's permission to break the ice on the purpose of the visit with an opening pantun in English.

"There is a rose in your garden that we see.
It would be proper to pollinate by our bee.
Let's share its beauty, if thou art agree,
And we have a bigger and happier family."

The hosts were impressed by the pantun in English, and they replied in a similar fashion.

"We welcome your visit with Muslim brotherhood.
We will convey our answer as soon as possible."

The ambassador delivered his thoughts on the matter. His close friend Ashman wanted to make Abdul Aziz's daughter his legally wedded wife. As a token of appreciation and promise to take care of Azmah, the ambassador showed a transfer form for a transfer of property to Azmah, which was a double-storey link house in Subang Jaya, with an estimated value close to one million. She could put pen to paper on the transfer if a gentleman's agreement could be reached on this matter.

"Mr. Aziz, I would very much like to see this proposal be a success, and on a personal note, I would like to invite both of you as a special guests to our beautiful country in the Gulf," the ambassador told the hosts.

Azmah's father nodded with a smile and replied, "Thank you very much for your generosity of the invitation. We shall consider it and would get back to you on this matter."

There were smiles accompanied by light laughter as the conversation got underway, and before long they conversed on the political scenarios in West Asia. Tea was served to the foreign dignitaries as the host extended his hospitality. Azmah was in her room and was told not to come out until the guests left.

Towards the end of the visit, the ambassador touched on the issue again as a reminder that he needed an answer to convey to his friend. His parting words were,

"Thanks for the warm hospitality and accommodating us. We sincerely hope that an answer in the affirmative is forthcoming."

Abdul Aziz replied, "Mr Ambassador, you are welcome, and we shall be in communication again."

With those words, it was time for the guest to leave and bid goodbye to all. The diplomatic car left the house and headed back to Kuala Lumpur with its escorts.

As the distinguished guest departed for Kuala Lumpur, Azmah was called and briefed. After hearing it, she cried with joy and hoped that there was a change of heart from her father. Her father then told her,

"I have not made my decision yet, but I am not easily swayed by such a delegation asking for your hand."

That statement was a shock to everyone in the house. Her mother and aunty said,

"Let Azmah make her own decision this time, because it concerns her life and future."

There was silence after that as everyone readied for the Magrib prayers. Azmah had high hopes.

Back in Kuala Lumpur, Ashman visited the ambassador's residence in Ampang for a firsthand account of what had transpired at the meeting. He had dinner as a guest of the ambassador and was briefed.

"What do you think of my chances?" asked Ashman.

The ambassador replied in a soft tone,

"I think it is fifty-fifty. Her father was non-committal on the matter, but he told us that he would contact me on the matter."

By now Ashman understood and told himself,

"That crafty old man is up to his tricks again." Soon after dinner, he excused himself and thanked the ambassador.

"Thank you once again, Your Excellency, for your help and assistance. May Allah repay your kindness."

Ashman went back home with mixed feeling. He later did some soul searching after his midnight prayers. Was his move to send in a Trojan horse in the form of high-powered delegation effective in overcoming the arrogant and incorrigible Abdul Aziz? The question left him dwelling in search of a solution.

He remembered in the old Malay Negeri Sembilan style that the male proposer would bring a group of well-equipped men and weapons to barge into the house belonging to the proposed bride, giving them an ultimatum to surrender and give away the daughter to the proposer, who would ask a hefty sum of money as a dowry and compensation, or else they would fight with whatever men and weapons were available. This was called the Serah method, but unfortunately it had not been practised of late. It was wishful thinking by Ashman because he was back to the drawing board for the next course of action should the delegation fail.

Ashman did not give up easily if obstacles come along his way. He was known for his perseverance and patience, which were the hallmarks of his character. This high-powered delegation was also unprecedented in the Malay culture, and if successful, it would go down in history. His determination showed no boundaries in the pursuit for Azmah, who meant everything to him. That reminded him of the evergreen song by Neil Sedaka, "You Mean Everything to Me", and he sang that song to lighten one of his darkest hours.

Chapter 19

A Demon in Pantomime

The time frame given by Abdul Aziz was "as soon as possible", but it did not indicate a fixed time, so Ashman had to keep his fingers crossed while hoping for the favourable answer. In the interim, he kept in communication with Amri and Amran not only about their mum but also on their own well-being. He was kept abreast on the latest developments, especially on Azmah, who was essentially placed on house arrest. On this subject, her two sons felt that their mum should not be subject to such humiliating treatment, and both of them hinted that their mum should be returning home to Kota Damansara and lead a normal life as any other widow, not be placed in her father's house in Seremban some eighty kilometres away.

Ashman told them, "If the women NGO were to bring up the issue of this confinement, or house arrest – or more accurate, false imprisonment – then your grandpa would be in deep trouble for flouting the law."

Amran agreed with him and replied,

"Yes, Uncle Ash. I would go along with you on that, and we would do our part in securing the release of our beloved mum."

Ashman then asked them, "Do you miss your mum?"

"Of course we do," they said.

Ashman told them,

"Uncle Ash does not have a locus standee as yet, but both of you do, and you could take up the issue."

In the evening, Amran called his grandma in Seremban, and they exchanged information on the latest development. Through her, Amran was able to convince her that their grandpa could be courting trouble on the false imprisonment matter.

"Yes, your grandpa must have gone bonkers over the matter, which I believe was not his own idea."

She assured Amran that she would do her utmost best to convince her husband on this, and they would hope for Azmah's release. That night before retiring to bed, their grandma had a heart-to-heart talk with her spouse on the matter, and it ran into the wee hours of the morning. Azmah slept a bit late, pondering her future. Rahimah Abdul Rahman promised her grandchildren that she would call them when a favourable result was forthcoming.

The following day during Friday prayers, as usual her father left the house for the mosque. Azmah took the opportunity to call Ashman by making a missed call, which was a signal that the coast was clear and that he could return the call. This was done to avoid detection on the records of outgoing calls from the house phone. He returned the call to his estranged bride in waiting, and a conversation followed, but it couldn't be too long because her crafty father would sometimes call back just to make sure everything was in order.

"I miss you a lot, Azmah," Ashman said.

Azmah was now ready to let the cat out of the bag, and she informed Ashman that her father had two gentlemen waiting in the fold, asking for her hand through him. One was a senior government servant with a grade of DG 54 who was an acquaintance of his father, and the other was a self-made businessman who could match what Ashman could offer in financial terms. Both were secret admirers of her.

"My goodness!" exclaimed Ashman.

That could explain why he was not high on Abdul Aziz's wish list. She added,

"I told my dad that you are my only love after the demise of Azman Ali, and I shall not accept any other man in my life."

Ashman was relieved to hear that and informed her that she needed to do more to persuade her father. She replied,

"Mum had a long talk with Dad last night, soon after Amran called her. We will have to wait a while, but I am already sick of staying here and told Dad that I wanted to go back home, come what may."

He advised her not to pre-empt or jeopardise his answer on the decision on the request from the delegation; otherwise, it could backfire.

"Yes, I will take your advice," she agreed.

The conversation lasted only twelve minutes, and Ashman prepared himself to go for Friday prayers. Now he could fathom why her father had acted in such an unbecoming and hostile manner. The irony was that during Azmah's first marriage, it was her own choice of a man she'd wanted, and now it was just the reverse. Azmah was known for her beauty and charm, and Ashman knew that because Azmah was stunningly beautiful, many men would see her as a perfect ten. For many, Azmah was Miss Malaysia material, and though she might not win the beauty pageant title, the runners-up position had always been her domain. Indeed, Azmah was a master of her craft that would make a life partner par excellence.

To put into layman's terms, a well-maintained, ten-year-old Mercedes was still preferred to a new, run-of-the-mill car. The equivalent in the Malay language was, "Hanya Jauhari Yang Mengenal Manikam." With all those superlatives showered upon her, there was no need for an explanation as to why many men were mesmerised and attracted to her.

A couple of days later after the advice by her mother, Azmah was allowed to return home to Kota Damansara to serve her "parole", and she took it with mixed feelings. Feeling traumatised was still fresh on her mind. She was sent back home by her father and mother, who stayed a couple old days at her house. Amran was delighted by the move and broke the news to Ashman, who was equally delighted.

"Thanks to Allah," Ashman said.

Amran said that they were now reunited as a family.

"Could it be a lull before a storm?" Ashman pondered.

As the hours and days went by, Ashman was waiting for an answer from her father through his friend, or via indirect reply through Azmah's family. He felt that it was like injury time, or added time in a football match, when the referee could blow the final whistle to end the game at any time. It had been nine days since the high-powered delegation was sent. For the record, Abdul Aziz did not speak to him even over the phone, and both of them caught glimpses of each other during the special prayers at Azmah's house during the bereavement of Azman Ali. Other than that, Abdul Aziz refused to speak to Ashman, even over the phone. This was unbecoming in the culture of Malay society, which held in high esteem such etiquette and manners. Azmah also tried to play down the behaviour of her father, but without much success. Little did Abdul Aziz realised that he would be killing the goose that laid the golden egg via his high-handed treatment of her.

The other piece of good news was that Azmah was given back her cell phone, but with a changed number. It was another thankless job for her to update the information inside her cell phone. There was no word whatsoever that she could call him. However, she took it in stride and equally hoped that her father's decision on Ashman's request would be a favourable one.

That night Ashman's ambassador friend called up Abdul Aziz, asking for news on the matter.

"I hope there is some favourable news for me to relay to my friend, Mr Abdul Aziz."

As a man of a few words, Abdul Aziz replied,

"I am still thinking about the matter and will reply in a couple of days."

The ambassador ended the conversation by saying,

"Very well, Mr. Abdul Aziz. We shall wait. Once again, thank you very much."

The following morning, Abdul Aziz left for Seremban with her mother, and Azmah was left in her house in Kota Damansara with Amri and Amran. She was about to restart her normal life, but some scars remained in her heart. Meanwhile, she tried to settle down in a gradual manner, and she called Ashman for the first time since coming back.

Ashman was delighted and joyful upon receiving the call.

"Take it easy, dear. You need some rest. Do what you like in your leisure time, even if you wish to cook some simple dishes."

Those comforting words were music to her ears, and she replied,

"Thank you, Ash. I know you will be around for me. Amri and Amran have found more time to be with me now that I am here."

"I am glad to hear that, and I wish you speedy recovery so that you are back on your feet again. Then we take off from where we stopped."

Before ending the conversation, she told him, "Thank you for your patience, Ash. I love you more each day."

Back in Seremban, Abdul Aziz was ready to drop the bombshell. True to form, he acted like a puppet on a string with hidden hands at work. That night he called up the ambassador and said that the request from Ashman to marry his daughter was not considered. He gave no reasons for the rejection. The ambassador was startled and speechless; he hadn't expected this kind of answer from Azmah's father, and he pondered whether he should call Ashman instantly to relay the massage or wait till the following day. After a while, he thought that he would wait to the following day to break this news.

Even without a clue of what was going around, Ashman found it difficult to sleep, but he did perform the early morning Tahajud prayers and then managed to catch some sleep.

The ambassador used caution and polished words so that Ashman would not be shocked upon hearing the answer. This time Ashman was prepared to hear the answer, and because time was of the essence, he could gauge the answer. Upon getting the answer through the ambassador, he was quiet and told his friend,

"Thank you very much for the help and kind hospitality over the matter. I take it with an open heart."

Now he could recall what he felt the other day upon the return of Azmah to Kota Damansara: it was too early for him to rejoice because it could be a lull before the storm.

In the afternoon, he rushed to Azmah's house to break the news and pay her a visit. Upon arrival, everything seemed quiet, and Azmah welcomed him to the living room of the house. Both were looking at each other and were speechless for a while. Ashman told her,

"You seemed to know the answer."

In a soft tone she replied,

"Yes. Dad called me early in the morning and told me."

In order to comfort her, he said,

"I knew when the ambassador called me that I'd expected this answer. Anyway, let us relax for a while till I think of a further step towards our course of action."

Ashman didn't stay long at her house and told her that he would have to leave because he had other matters to attend to. With a tinge of sadness, she waved goodbye to Ashman while tears flowed from her eyes.

Back home, Ashman, who was not known to throw tantrums, cursed Abdul Aziz.

"If Egypt had Alexander the Great, Kurdistan had Saladin the Great or Sallahudin Al Ahyubi, and Russia had Peter the Great, then Malaysia has Abdul Aziz the Great – the greatest Malaysian who has ever lived!"

Chapter 20

Avoiding a Waterloo

Ashman was now back to the drawing board. It looked like he was caught between the devil and the deep blue sea. Because the Trojan horse method was not a success, he consulted his close friends and relatives on what his next course of action should be. Most of them were sympathetic over the matter but could not offer the kind of advice he required. Others said, "Forget about her and find someone else."

He was quick to rebut,

"We made a vow at Jabbal Rahmah that come what may, we shall not split and till death do us part."

One of his friends said,

"Are you going to live up to your vow when matters doesn't work for both of you? It's like sailing in turbulent waters, where you might capsize."

Reluctantly he agreed and told him,

"It just like walking on thin ice, but don't skiing champions perform on thin ice?"

For a while he pondered that there was some truth in it. Others would say,

"There are many other ladies that Allah has created, and ones without any baggage." Another added,

"If you wish, I have a few candidates for you to consider."
In an instance, Ashman replied,
"I've had enough of Nur Nilam Sari and the like." He later politely told them,
"Let me do some soul searching, and I'll let you know later."
Mohamed Chan also called him to find out the latest developments. Ashman asked, "Would it be proper to file this matter in the Syariah court for wali enggan, or guardian's refusal to allow his daughter to marry a man of her choice?"
Chan told him that it would be a little unethical for him after asking for Azmah's hand and being turned down. He added, "It's not actually a 'sour grape' move, but legally you could do that, and eventually the Syariah court could well rule in your favour."
Ashman though that by doing so, the implications were too great.

1. Azmah would be disowned by him.
2. They would have some troubled times without Abdul Aziz's blessings.
3. There'd be negative gossip from nosey people around.

All in all, it would revolve on matters of one's pride. For Ash, it could be seen as accomplishing Mission Impossible that few would undertake. The end result was about a happy marriage. However, he kept this option at bay.

In the meantime, he occasionally called Azmah by cell phone to be in contact with her and relay his thoughts. From the way the conversation went, Azmah was depressed, and at times she had difficulties sleeping. He advised that she perform special prayers before retiring to bed. Occasionally her father dropped in at her house to have a look, and her health was affected: she was more depressed and felt worse by the day. Her two sons were not too pleased with the actions of their grandfather, and their relationship deteriorated. At one juncture, Amran had to take his mum to a rejuvenation clinic for treatment. Ashman was there at the clinic to show support and settle the bills. Up to this point, Ashman had never touched her on bare skin, and he only shook her hand or gave a helping hand to walk her to the car.

Azmah's condition, which by now was not in the best health, was noticed by her siblings and close friends who visited her at her house. However, she managed simple cooking, and at other times she called for pizza delivery. Ashman would buy food for her and deliver it to her house a few times a week, but she would not stay for long. By now Azmah had already employed an Indonesian maid to help her with the housework and keep her company. Her health condition was kept secret from her father until he could see for his own eyes. She thought that would be better than reporting her general state of health. Amri and Amran were back frequently from their colleges to be with their mum. Thanks to their late father, they'd saved enough money to buy them motorcars.

Since the drama at Kangar, Perlis, which was now five months ago, Azmah had lost seven kilos, and her BMI now was at a low 22.5, lower than the ideal number of 25.0 that she had maintained before. Her father didn't notice this, but her mother did, and she could understand why. In the interim, she received a few telephone calls from the officers (but not a gentleman) who were her father's choice. They called her just to say hello and to break the ice. She politely told him that she wasn't interested in knowing anyone else, and she requested they maintain a distance. One of them, a senior government officer, came along with her father for one of the visits, but she stayed in her room and didn't bother to receive them. In one instance, she told her father,

"Even if you force me to marry one of them, I will not consummate the marriage. I will get a chastity belt for that purpose."

She was known to be headstrong over certain matters.

Ashman was in a fix about whether to continue the Syariah court reporting of guardian's refusal or to have a plan B by looking at other options. The idea of waiting for her father to ascend the celestial abode was unthinkable because life and death was a matter for Allah to decide. What made him go for Azmah was that other women did not fit his description, or the chemistry was not right. Even the ladies whom he met prior to knowing Azmah let him down badly or failed miserably when it mattered most.

Back home, Ashley, then about to enter college, would occasionally ask him whether he had found the right candidate. His answer was that the matter was still not resolved. At last he confided to Ashley what had happened on the fateful day in Kangar, Perlis. Ashley was sad and bitterly disappointed about the debacle, and she told herself,

"Why would anyone with a sane mind do anything like that?"

She didn't tell her mum about it to save the family's embarrassment.

While the saga of guardian's refusal remaining unchanged, Ashman thought that he had to do something to salvage lost pride, and he asked for opinions from his siblings. Most of them thought that should he pursue the reporting to the Syariah court, it would regain him and his family some dignity and respect whilst at the same time uphold the rule of Islamic law.

"But wouldn't that be a tit for tat kind of reaction?" he asked himself.

"It all depends on what you want out of it," said one family relation.

He told them,

"If I don't pursue the matter on guardian's refusal, it is like throwing in the towel."

He told them a little bit of history: Napoleon Bonaparte was finally defeated in the Battle of Waterloo and was exiled. Ash's objective was not to accept defeat and leave Azmah in the wilderness of suffering from the failed mission. There were no two ways about it: either he'd go to the Syariah court, or he could lose Azmah forever. Ashman did not want to concede defeat, at least not for the time being.

That night he called up Azmah and told her briefly what had transpired at the brainstorming session that he'd had with his siblings and close relations. As expected, Azmah was speechless, but they were to meet the following day at the rejuvenation clinic for a follow-up treatment. Azmah tried to look good, but signs of her instability of mind and health could not be hidden. There were counselling sessions for her as part of the treatment. Of late, she began to forget certain events and had a loss of memory. Those were factors that worried Ashman; the uncalled for and uncivilised actions of Abdul Aziz were now showing signs of her long-term suffering. After the treatment, they had lunch together for the first time since the Kangar drama, and Ashman took her to the Hornbill Restaurant. They managed to catch up some lost time, and it looked as if nothing had happened to them.

Back home, Ashman knew that he had to make a decision on the next step to take if he really wanted to succeed in getting Azmah as his life partner. He gathered a few close relations and discussed his next move, leaving no stone unturned. He wanted to go for broke like crossing the Rubicon, so he might as well proceed with taking it to Syariah court for guardian's refusal. That night he her performed special prayers for the occasion, seeking direction and guidance. It wasn't an easy decision for him to make, but in the end such an action was inevitable.

The following day, Ashman consulted Mohamed Chan on the matter and relayed his thoughts and plan. In return, Chan offered him some insights into it, and the path was now clear for Ashman to proceed. Soon after that, he called on Azmah to explain the proposed move, and he wanted her to fill out the necessary application forms for solemnisation of the marriage in Selangor.

Azmah was lost for words on hearing that and kept her silence; she wasn't in a position to disagree or agree over the matter. She told him,

"Do what you think that is best for us, Ash."

He replied, "Relax, my dear. What is good for the goose is good for the gander."

On hearing that Azmah told him,

"You really made my day, Ash."

"I am glad to be of help to you today, and I shall bring the forms to you tomorrow once I've download them from the website."

In the afternoon the following day, Ashman made a short visit to Azmah's house to have the forms signed. It was a hot and sunny afternoon as he entered her house, and coincidentally Amran was with her. This provided the opportunity for him to brief Amran over the matter, and the son fully understood and supported it. They had coffee during the short encounter, and for the first time in many months, Azmah looked cheerful and sanguine. Still, traces of her sickness were visible to observant eyes. Ashman thanked both of them and requested they perform special prayers on the matter in order to have Allah's blessings. He then left the house on a mission.

As he drove past the main road junction, he witnessed an unidentified car heading towards Azmah's house. Azmah then texted him over the cell phone that her father had dropped in unexpectedly. Ashman told himself,

"That was a close shave. My goodness, the wily fox could sniff something that was going to work against him. Anyway, thank God that I managed to avoid him."

He then told her, "It's okay, my dear. I managed to steer away from the situation in the nick of time. Thank Allah for that."

Those words were comforting to her because she had to entertain her father, who'd made a surprise visit under the pretext of wanting to visit an old friend at the university hospital in PJ.

Her father told her, "I just want to make sure that everything is okay with you, Azmah. If you are all right, I will return to Seremban in the evening."

Azmah replied,

"I am okay, Dad, but why didn't you bring Mum along?"

His reply was, "Your mum is as busy as ever."

Her father was about to leave for Seremban in the evening, after having coffee with traditional Malay cakes, which was their family's tradition for years. Azmah told her father that she wanted to discuss one matter with him. Abdul Aziz looked in astonishment and asked her,

"What is it, my daughter?"

Without further delay, she gave him a brown envelope for him to go through. By the time her father set his eyes on the papers, she told him,

"Dad, I would like you to give your signature as consent for me to get married to Ashman. If you love your daughter so much, as you have always claimed to others, and if do not want me to suffer, then do the needful."

The strong words that came from his only daughter were unexpected to him, and after a moment, he looked at her and replied,

"I will not sign this now."

Azmah added, "If you don't, then shall get my brother, Amin, or Uncle Abdullah to sign it as guardian, with or without your agreement."

Abdul Aziz was dumbfounded but cynically told her,

"Did Ashman teach you this?"

In a hurry, he then told her,

"Not now, dear. I am in a hurry."

He went to his motorcar and drove away without bidding goodbye to his daughter.

After nightfall, she called Ashman over the cell phone and related to him what had transpired. He said,

"Not to worry, dear. I am glad that you showed what you were made of. Be assured that I shall proceed with the plan.

I shall fill up the guardian's refusal forms and let you sign them."

With the latest development, Ashman rushed to Azmah's house to get her to sign the guardian's refusal form after dinner. He arrived at nine o'clock and went into the house accompanied by one of his aunties, for fear that some nosey neighbours might report to the Religious Department a "close proximity" offence under Syariah law. His moves and visits to Azmah's house were carefully deciphered to avoid any uncalled-for incidents. He introduced his aunty before entering the house. After getting Azmah's signature, he left, and everything was over within ten minutes, including coffee.

The following day, Ashman took a day off from the office to visit the State Religious Department. He was accompanied by his legal adviser, Mohamed Chan, who had been his mentor over these matters. What seemed to be a simple and straightforward matter in the beginning had turned out to be a very complicated and legal matter as long as Abdul Aziz was around. The episode of a legal battle was about to begin as both of them stepped into the Religious Department and met the officer in charge to start the proceedings against Abdul Aziz. Before leaving the office, both of them were assured by the officer that he would make his best endeavours to expedite the proceedings. The officer added,

"The guardian will be summoned to court to explain the reasons for refusal. He'll be given three chances to attend court. If he's in default, the court will decide on the application of marriage."

With those words, Ashman and Chan left the Religious Department with some optimism.

As Ashman was descending the steps of the Religious Department office, he told himself,

"Whatever the outcome of this long-running saga, I shall write a book on this and highlight Malay and Muslim society regarding such major misdemeanours and atrocities."

He then added,

"Enough is enough. Society must be educated of their rights, which have been denied them for so long by way of literature, other than going through Syariah lawyers, or the Syariah Legal Assistance Bureau for those who can't afford lawyer fees."

They reached their cars, and Ashman thanked Mohamed Chan. Before they split, he managed to get Azmah on the line and briefed her on what took place at the Religious Department. She was a bit relieved that their application had received due attention from the authorities.

After one week, Ashman received a copy of the summons. Presumably Abdul Aziz had received the same because it was to be acknowledged receipt by the recipient. The date of the proceeding was one week from then, and Ashman was very eager for his case to be heard. On that Monday, as fixed by the Syariah court, Azmah's father did not attend court, but he called the court officer that he was not well and would produce a medical certificate. Ashman expected this kind of delay tactic. He then called Azmah to inform her that the proceeding was postponed due to her father's absence. Deep inside, Ashman was furious about the cheap tricks, but he was able to hide all the frustrations, and he took it in stride. He told himself,

"Still waters run deep – it's is an apt description of Abdul Aziz."

Both parties had to wait for the second hearing, which would come in another three or four weeks. Meanwhile, Azmah called her mother to inform her what had happened. She also hoped that her mother would be able to assist by coaxing her father into approving her request; at times, he seemed to have a soft spot for his wife. Unless hidden hands were at work, there was always the slightest chance of a reluctant agreement. Her mother said that the hidden hands were still active in influencing her father on those matters. During this period, Azmah was not in communication with her father, and as expected a cold war developed between father and daughter. Her mother tried to be the mediator among the two, but with little success.

Life went on as usual for Azmah and Ashman, and they were still in contact with one another. Their meetings were restricted during this interim period because both wanted a smooth and trouble-free period. One day Ashman called on Mohamed Chan and exchanged ideas on what would be his next move should the court decide against him, but Chan advised him to keep his fingers crossed and not pre-empt the court's decision.

The second call for guardian's refusal to Abdul Aziz was made, and a week's notice was given to both parties. On hearing that, Azmah called her mother to coax her father to turn up for the appointment. Against all odds, Abdul Aziz turned up for the proceedings without a personal attorney. In Syariah court there was a tense atmosphere like at a football match. The proceeding would commence at ten in the morning, and both parties were present half an hour beforehand. Abdul Aziz seemed to avoid Ashman in the crowd, and even when they entered the courtroom, Abdul Aziz didn't care to look at Ashman, waiting until their turn was called. Azmah was not required to be present until the court decided to call her at a later date.

The presiding judge entered the courtroom, and their proceeding was first on the agenda. Mohamed Chan, representing Ashman, took the floor and tendered the notice to the judge before commencement. The judge asked Abdul Aziz his reasons for refusing to allow his daughter to marry Ashman Mohamed Ali. Abdul Aziz stood up and explained the reasons for his refusal. He then took out a paper from his pocket and read from it.

1. Azmah and Ashman tried to marry away, without my consent, sometime back. I managed to intercept the proposed marriage solemnisation in Perlis in the wee hours of the morning and took back my daughter. It was very unbecoming for both of them.

2. Following the aborted attempt to solemnise the marriage in Perlis, Ashman sent a high-powered delegation to my residence in Seremban to ask for my permission to marry Azmah. I refuse because I had in mind whom she should marry.

Those were the two reasons Abdul Aziz gave, which were deemed to be weak in form and substance by Mohamed Chan. The judge asked Chan to put forth his reasons on behalf of his client, Ashman. Chan took the floor and asked the court to consider the following before a decision was made. He reiterated that his client should be granted the permission to marry Azmah. Chan told the packed courtroom the following:

1. His client, Ashman Mohamed Ali, and Azmah Abdul Aziz had, prior to their trip to Perlis, sought permission from Abdul Aziz for consent to marry his daughter. The father refused and didn't want to meet his client, let alone entertain any meeting or discussion on this matter.
2. His client had known Azmah after the demise of her husband, and love blossomed between the two. Both her grown-up sons were in favour of their marriage.
3. The court should consider all this and allow their marriage to proceed. One of the tenets in Islam advocates marriage and strongly prohibited couples from committing adultery.
4. In addition to that, Azmah had not been in the best of health and was feeling deeply depressed after her father's refusal to allow her to marry Ashman.
5. Unless Abdul Aziz was deeply indebted financially or otherwise to any of the two men, explaining why he wanted to give away his daughter to a man of his choice, then he was being grossly unfair. This was like the story in the Malay film by P. Ramlee, *Bujang Lapok*, where the same thing was done, resulting in the woman trying to commit suicide.
6. As a widow with two grown-up sons, this would be Azmah's second marriage with a man of her choice. Her first marriage was also a man of her choice.

After hearing from both sides of the divide, the presiding judge adjourned the proceeding and said that the decision would be made in due course. On hearing that, Abdul Aziz made a quick dash to his motorcar and headed home. Ashman looked at Chan and wondered what the outcome would be. His attorney advised him that he has a good chance of the decision granted in his favour, if such proceedings in the past were a precedent. Both of them spent another half hour discussing the matter at the café of the courthouse. Ashman took the opportunity to call Azmah and related to her what had happened. He advised her to be patient because he had a feeling it could go their way.

One week passed, and still there was no news about it and Ashman instructed Chan to call up the Syariah court to check on the latest development. They were the informally told that Ashman failed to get the court's permission to marry Azmah, and this decision would be reverted in writing in the next couple of days. Chan relayed the news to Ashman. Ash kept his cool and relayed the news to Azmah, who received it with tears. She was near fainting, but she had expected it and did not want to make her feelings known earlier. However, Ashman assured her that there was still a chance of a review, and he would discuss it with Chan.

Up to then, Azmah was not being called for her to explain what she felt about the matter. She told them through phone,

"Where is justice, which is not only to be seen but done?" as she burst into tears, She continued,

"Don't tell me these people are only good at snooping couples even though they are on social visits and arresting them under the pretext of "close proximity. Is this how Islamic laws are being dispensed with?"

She was later calmed by Ashman who used his good inter-personal skills and managed to bring her back to her senses.

"Cool down my dear, Allah is with us".

"We lost a battle but not the war".

He then added, "It's just a temporary setback. Remember Istanbul 2005 when Liverpool FC staged a dramatic comeback to win the European Champions League trophy after being 3-0 down against AC Milan?

He then asked, "Do you believe in miracles?"

"Castles are built in the air!"

"Remember the vows we made at Jabbal Rahmah in Mekkah? This is part of it."

Certainly Ashman was in his element that saved her from further damage. Azmah was able to sleep well after the counselling from him.

That night, Ashman did some soul searching. His gut feeling suspected that something had gone wrong. He then made a point to call Chan's office in the evening and relay his concerns.

"Chan, could you do some homework on the presiding judge? I believe there is some connection with Abdul Aziz. They could be distantly related or have some kind of friendship between them that resulted in a decision in Abdul Aziz's favour."

Chan the told him,

"Okay, my friend, I will do that. But it could take some time, and time is of the essence here because the decision will be conveyed soon."

"Never mind, Chan. We'll try this to get some positive results," Ashman said. He was not yet ready to throw in the towel.

Within a couple of days, Chan found out that there was some relationship between: Abdul Aziz knew the father of the judge. Acting on Ashman's instructions, Chan set to apply to the court for a new presiding judge to hear the matter because there was a conflict of interests. Such matters were common in civil and criminal cases, but very rarely did it happen in Syariah court. The following day, Chan made an application, which caused a cry amongst those concerned. Finally the news broke to Abdul Aziz, who did not take kindly to issues that had affected his credibility and image. But the law was still the law, and it had to be respected by all.

It took three days for the appeal to be decided, and Ashman and Azmah waited eagerly with high hopes. The decision came suddenly that the court felt despite a little conflict of interest, the presiding judge did not err over the matter, and the decision stood. In the space of three days, there was ecstasy and then agony for Ashman and Azmah, who felt they were cheated of a decision in their favour. On the other side, Abdul Aziz was happy with his personal victory on the matter, and he arrogantly told his close friends and colleagues that he ultimately won the saga over the matter; he maintained his stand was correct all along. For Abdul Aziz it was, "Winner takes all and losers standing small", like the song from ABBA pop group of the seventies.

Ashman was still licking his wounds. Azmah had deteriorated in her health since her abduction with bouts of depression. She told her sons,

"After losing my husband, now I am losing my beloved Ashman. Oh, God, what have I done to deserve all this?"

Amri and Amran were there to comfort her and told her mum,

"Rome is not built in one day, you need to be patient".

Both of them were now a source of inspiration to her throughout the long road of her journey to be a legally wedded wife again. She then told Ashman,

"I am tired of all these non-sensible actions. I need a break. Let's go somewhere, like Perth or Bali."

Ashman told her, "I had been thinking of such places for our honeymoon, but not right now"

He had thoughts of a honeymoon in Perth, which would start with a night river cruise at the Swan River, seafood dinner at Freemantle, shopping at the Harbour Town and taking a boat ride at Mandurrah or known as little Venice of Australia. Azmah felt relieved on hearing his plans for their honeymoon. More important than that she did remember Ashman's advice:

"Never give up! Even Satan would never give up in tempting Adam's children until the end of time."

Chapter 21

Riding into the Sunset

"**N**ight and day, you are the one." – Cole Porter

The lyric from Cole Porter was a fitting description of the unwavering love of Ashman to Azmah that knew no boundaries. To date, there were lessons learnt. They took a cue from Napoleon Bonaparte, who was finally defeated in the Battle of Waterloo after so many attempts to score a victory. Alas, Ashman was not the knight in shining armour that most people wanted him to be in his relentless pursuit of winning over Azmah. He was surely a dour fighter who would not concede defeat so easily. In contrast, his nemesis, Abdul Aziz, was unrelenting is his efforts to derail him. What could be more embarrassing for an engineer specialising in railway construction than to be derailed by the efforts of Abdul Aziz? To top it all, an insidious campaign was made some time ago by Abdul Aziz to discredit Ashman. This paradox was a cold war that developed between the two, and though it did not amount to a holy crusade, it was almost unprecedented in Malaysian culture to date.

Ashman did a post-mortem on the tragic events. He was a frustrated man who dreaded what would happen in the end. The trial and tribulations took more than six years of his second bachelorhood, and he discovered that even crossing the Rubicon did not help him. Like in football, he discovered that

1. There was no level playing field for him.
2. As he was about to score, they shifted the goal posts.
3. The buyout clause didn't work for him this time, or someone had outbid him even though he was the first to register and be accepted.

In addition, he discovered that when it came to love, the best man did not always win. Money and influence would be incessantly important towards the success of securing a woman as a legally wedded wife. Though he had mastered the book *Men Are from Mars, Women Are from Venus* by Dr John Gray, which was about the husband and wife relationship, it did little to help him on the success of his mission.

Throughout the period, he was more than a shoulder to lean on for Azmah during their courtship days. All in all, he was a mentor to her, and she looked upon him as a guiding light.

As the twilight zone loomed over the horizon, it looked like Ashman and Azmah were not going to ride towards the sunset together as husband and wife, but as close friends and a loving couple who understood one another but lived separately. His greatest fear was that Azmah might not be able to ride through the sunset. It might turn out to be the longest day in their lives because both were tired and weary of the saga. Azmah was now in her late forties, and Ashman was in his middle fifties; once again, time was of the essence. With all the high hopes, aspirations, and great plans for a happy ending, they discovered that their golden days during courtship were to come to an end.

1. The Indian summer was a short-lived one, with their limited company restricting their meeting each other.
2. The high hopes during performing the pilgrimage together and their prayers at prescribed sacred places were severely put to test after their arrival back in Malaysia.
3. Their hopes for a marriage solemnisation were dashed in a commando-style abduction, and another two attempts failed miserably.
4. The only hope now was to take Azmah out of Malaysia under some pretext and solemnise their marriage in a foreign land, but she was not in a position to travel.

The focus of attention was now on Azmah, who didn't look good, and her health deteriorated because she had developed a sudden lapse of memory. Azmah was fully depressed as the events didn't go the way she wanted. She went for a medical check-up, and the specialist confirmed that Alzheimer's had quietly crept upon her. Most of her close friends were able to notice it, particularly Amri and Amran, and of course Ashman. Her sons were not too happy with the state of their mother's health, but Abdul Aziz was quick to shift the blame to Ashman as the root cause of the problem. Amri and Amran were not born yesterday and were not fooled by their grandfather. Their dislike for their grandfather soon developed into hatred. Ashman did not want to add salt to the wound, and he advised the boys to be patient and treat it as a test from Allah.

Azmah's close friend Zaini would regularly check up on her to provide comfort and consolation, and so did her other close relations. Her mother was equally disturbed over her deteriorating state of health, but Abdul Aziz stood firm on his decision, stubborn to the core. He looked more like another monster created by Frankenstein who was now adept at skinning a dead cat not just once but twice.

Motherly instincts made Rahimah regularly visit Azmah, but it was Ashman's presence and great care that comforted Azmah. She said,

"If only Ash would move to the nearby link house, which was vacant for some time. How wonderful it would be."

His reply was, "That would be great, but not at this time. The situation does not permit me right now, and your father might get a court order restraining me from moving nearby, knowing the man he is."

He added, "The best solution is for me to move into your house, or you move to my house as a legally wedded couple."

Amri and Amran played their parts in keeping their mother happy and feeling comfortable. They looked at Ashman as a fatherly figure when seeking advice. Every now and then, they would take their mother for lunch or high tea at her favourite places, and Ashman would be there to join them and pick up the bill. Of particular interest was the Hornbill Restaurant, which drew nostalgic memories of their rendezvous. At times they went for a movie at the nearby cinema; the James Bond movies were their top choice. Under such circumstances, almost everything went smoothly in their daily lives except for the last piece of the jigsaw puzzle, which was held by Abdul Aziz.

Suddenly Azmah's health took a turn for the worse. She had to be wheeled off in an ambulance to the Pantai Medical Centre. Amri was not around, and only Amran and her mother were there to help. She had been admitted to this hospital some twenty-one years ago for the miscarriage of her first child, and now she was admitted for another miscarriage: a gross miscarriage of justice for not being allowed to marry the man of her choice. It was a shattering moment for Azmah. She was drowning in her sorrows, and anyone could easily notice it.

Ashman was on a working visit in Jakarta for a project. On receipt of the news, he managed to cut short his visit, and he returned home and visited Azmah. On reaching the ward, he crossed paths with Abdul Aziz, who didn't bother to look him in the face as he dashed to his car. Ashman told himself,

"What kind of a Muslim this man is. Even infidels don't react like this!"

Upon entering the room, was her mother sitting beside and reciting the Yaasin, which was a condensed version of the holy Koran. Though her condition had improved, the presence of Ashman really made the difference. She and her mother were delighted at his presence. Her mother told Ashman,

"She will be discharged in three days. She is too weak right now."

"Thank you, Auntie," was his reply. Azmah managed to put on a smile as the three were reunited, and they had lunch together, sharing a large size pizza.

Two days later, the specialist who attended to Azmah re-examined her and told Ashman and Rahimah that she was suffering from bouts of depression. Such situations could worsen in the near future.

"Try to keep her happy, and please her in any way you can. Her Alzheimer's is still there and hasn't improved."

The specialist added, "She needs treatment from time to time. When it comes, get her admitted as soon as possible."

Ashman asked the doctor,

"When will she be discharged?"

"If her condition remains stable, perhaps by tomorrow", was the answer.

However, the patient had other ideas, wanting to stay as long as it was required. Ashman asked her, "Are you not homesick, my dear?" There was silence on her part, and it was another night that her mother was at the ward to keep her company.

Back home in Kota Damansara, Azmah was thinking that she needed a place to temporarily call home. Mother Rahimah could not stay in Kota Damansara with her for long because her father needed her at their house in Seremban. Abdul Aziz could not stay at her daughter's house for long, only for a couple of days, and Azmah did not want to stay in Seremban. She discussed the matter with her two sons, who couldn't shuttle back and forth from their house and college. She was left with only her Indonesian maid, who took weekends off. Ashman could not be there with her all the time. Zaini dropped in from Perlis occasionally. Azmah then called upon Ashman to discuss the matter with her.

Ashman came over for evening coffee to discuss the matter, with Azmah and Amran. Due to the nature of her sickness, and given that she needed someone to look after her. She suggested to them,

"My dear Ashman and my beloved son, after careful thought and due consideration, I have decided to temporarily stay at the dementia nursing home, near Teluk Panglima Garang in Banting, some seventy-five kilometres from here."

"What!" exclaimed Amran.

"Relax, my son, this is for my best interests, and everyone else's too. All of you can visit me on a weekly basis or any other time suitable for you."

Amran was close to tears, but Ashman was able to cool him down like a paternal father who understood his child. Ashman then told Azmah,

"If that is your wish, we will respect it and carry it out. Your wish is our command." On hearing that, Azmah looked a little happy.

The following day, Ashman called her mother and spoke to her father as well, informing them of her decision to stay at the dementia nursing home in Banting on the advice of her specialist doctor. Both her parents were taken by surprise, but Rahimah was more understanding of the two and gave her blessings to Azmah. On this matter, Abdul Aziz eventually gave way to her daughter's wish. Amri was soon to learn of his mother's decision, and he accepted it with some reluctance. Amri and Amran looked at Ashman like their foster father. Ashman was happy to act as their mentor in the absence of the boys' father. As everyone connected to Azmah learned of her plan, they wished her well. It was Ashman, again unknown to the rest, who would foot the bill for Azmah's stay.

The following week, with all the necessary papers sorted out, Azmah was given a touching send-off by Ashman, Amri, and Amran. Ashman came over to their house in Kota

Damansara, and all of them went in Ashman's new Mercs C Class, with Amran at the driver's seat. Azmah sat in the rear seat with Ashman. Throughout the journey to Teluk Panglima Garang, they were quiet except for a few questions from the boys on the direction of travel which Ashman guided them. They stopped for some refreshments at Klang before continuing to the nursing home. It was a breeze of a journey in the new German marque. Ashman bought this new motorcar for the sake of Azmah who always wanted one of her own.

They arrived at eleven in the morning, and after registration, Azmah was welcomed to the nursing home. All of them were introduced to the specialist doctor in charge. They were made comfortable by the home's fraternity, and Azmah looked more upbeat. She had her first lunch at the home, and she was joined by Ashman and her two sons. Her programme commenced after lunch, so the three of them bid her farewell with hugs and kisses from her sons. She waved goodbye as the motorcar pulled away from the nursing home.

In the evening, Ashman called her to check on her status and well-being. He was happy to note that she was well taken care of by the staff, and arrangements were made by her sons to visit her on weekends. Her parents visited her the following day and brought her favourite food. Not much conversation was made between them, but Azmah told her parents thanks. After two hours, her parents left.

The weekend after was a visit by her two sons, and in the evening Ashman paid her a visit and stayed till dusk. Then there was the usual farewell between Ashman and Azmah and she kissed his hand as a mark of respect.

Throughout her first month at the dementia nursing home, other close friends and relations visited her, including Zaini Harun. Life would not be the same for Azmah in the home, but at least she continued to receive the necessary treatment. The second month drew slightly fewer visitors, and the third month was almost the same as the second month. Ashman was in constant touch with her through the cell phone and made weekly visits, and so did Amri and Amran, though not at the same time. Everything seemed quiet for the family of Azmah. They had come to terms with her health.

Her condition then took a dent, and she was in a wheelchair because of weak knees. This made Ashman worried, but he steadfastly clung to his prayers to Allah, seeking the best. Her two sons were equally worried upon seeing her deterioration. On one of the visits, Ashman asked the specialist about her condition. The doctor explained it to him, but the worry kept coming to him.

Ashman was soon made to accept her worsening condition. She couldn't hide her forlorn expressions, but she managed a smile each time a visitor turned up. This was not the sunset that Ashman and Azmah had wanted, but they were still "together". As mentioned earlier, the condition of her health made Ashman worried, and he felt that they could not watch nor experience the sunset together in their lives.

One night after the usual nightly conversation with her, Ashman went to bed early and had a bad dream. He dreamt that he was in a Muslim cemetery at Bukit Kiara, Kuala Lumpur, walking around. He suddenly stumbled into the tombstone of a grave and noticed the engraving in the centre.

Azmah Abdul Aziz, 1966–2015

Immediately he woke up and performed the Tahajud, or special prayers, in the wee hours of the morning, seeking the best protection from Allah. After prayers, he tried to go back to sleep, but his eyes wouldn't close as he thought of the unthinkable. His gut feeling was that a premonition was hovering around his head regarding things to come.

Early in the morning after Subuh prayers, he was ready for the day. After an early breakfast of french toast and specially brewed coffee, he packed his executive briefcase. Instead of heading for the office, he texted the office that he wanted to take emergency leave. He headed towards Teluk Panglima Garang and didn't inform anyone about his intended visit to the nursing home. He hoped that his gut feeling was wrong and that he'd simply had a meaningless bad dream. Throughout the journey, he chanted special prayers with hopes that everything was all right.

He didn't even call Azmah while driving, but his driving did not reflect that he was in a hurry. His memories went back to the song. "This is My Prayer" that Azmah sang in their first karaoke meeting which was a very sad song and he wondered if another moment of truth was approaching by in whatever manner. Those lyrics were still fresh on his mind which read,

"This is my prayer",
"My silent prayer",
"All I wish for",
"On every star....",
"That he will care",
"Really care".

The song had such impact on him as prayers are part of his daily lives. He then tried to play down those memories related to it and for a while he was quiet hoping for the best. As he was about to arrive, the feeling of uneasiness crept into him, and he didn't know what was in store for him. Five minutes later, he made his much-awaited arrival. At 9.30 he called upon her to meet in the visitor's lounge.

There were no signs as yet of what was to come. Azmah wheeled herself to the visitor's lounge to meet her husband in waiting. As she approached him, after giving the sweetest smile of all time, she burst into tears. She stood up from her wheelchair and held him by the arms. The reunion was short-lived because she fell from his arms. He support her, and she was almost speechless. She looked pale, and her body was cold. In her dying breadth, she uttered.

"I love you, Ashman. Please take care of Amri and Amran."

Ashman was shell-shocked, and he held Azmah in his arms while signalling for help. He managed to ask her to chant her last prayers to Allah.

Soon after help came, Ashman looked at Azmah forlornly while she took her last breath and passed away peacefully in his lap. For the first and last time, Ashman kissed her on her cheek as a mark of respect to her. He couldn't withhold his tears as he witnessed his beloved take her last breadth, but he regained his composure soon after. He took out his cell phone, called her mother and sons, and informed them with deep regret that Azmah had been called to Allah just minutes ago.

The sweetest smile that Ashman had ever witnessed from Azmah three minutes ago proved to be her swansong smile. It was probably the most difficult hour of Ashman's life as the final curtain call was made in the most improbable place, a nursing home.

Not too long on hearing the news, nursing home residents gathered around and paid their last respects to her with flowers abound and condolence messages were put on the board which read,

"Rest in Peace, Azmah."

It was certainly an emotional and touching farewell to the golden girl from Batu Pahat. Her heroics and resilience in the wake of adversity is an icon for all women.

The End